MW00882580

Nate ROCKS the SCHOOL

Karen Pokras Toz

© 2013 by Karen Pokras Toz
All Rights Reserved

Published by

Grand Daisy Press

All rights reserved. No part of this publication may be reproduced, distributed, or transmitted in any form or by any means, including photocopying, recording, or other electronic or mechanical methods, without the prior written permission of the publisher, except in the case of brief quotations embodied in critical reviews and certain other noncommercial uses permitted by copyright law. For permission requests, please go to www.karentoz.com

*Disclaimer:*The characters in this novel are fictitious. Any resemblance to actual individuals is purely coincidental.

ISBN-10: 0984860878
ISBN-13: 978-0-9848608-7-6

Library of Congress Control No: 2013931288

For more information, please visit
www.karentoz.com

Edited by Melissa Ringsted of There For You Editing
Cover and Interior Design by BookStarter

Manufactured in the United States of America

Praise For Nate Rocks the School

"My eleven-year-old is always asking me when the next Nate Rocks book will be available. I have to admit that I love the series as much as he does! Nate Rocks the School puts the "fun" in fundraising!"

-Amanda Beatty Chambers, *Living, Learning, and Loving Life*

"Toz has a good cast of characters in this middle school series and has the ability to get readers of all ages involved in her stories. "Nate Rocks the School" is fun and well-worth your time."

— Jack Magnus, *Readers' Favorite*

"Nate Rocks the School by Karen Pokras Toz, another fun must read for you and your 7 to 12 year old. I had so much fun reading about Nate and his classmate's fundraiser mishaps and being part of Nate's daydreams. The ending is spectacular."

— Wendy Nystrom, author of *James Saves the Moon* and *Helga Returns*

"Two things are guaranteed whenever reading a Nate Rocks book; you will love where his awesome imagination takes you and you will find yourself smiling the whole way through. In Nate Rocks the School author Karen Toz continues her streak of winning Middle-Grade books. Pick up this series today to introduce your kids to a love of reading! As for me, I'm ready for Nate to Rock New York next!"

— Stacey Rourke, *Author of The Gryphon Series*

"... a great book to have in schools and for children to share at home with their parents. [T]his is truly an adventurous, exciting, interesting and fun story to read."

— Darin Godby, *Readers' Favorite*

To my incredible family,
with much love and admiration.
You all rock.

Chapter 1

Buildings collapse to the ground as the giant robot pushes its way through the dark city streets. The road crumbles underneath the massive beast's every move. Frightened citizens have all been evacuated and are hiding inside City Hall's basement, normally a secure refuge during even the worst situations.

"Nate," the mayor pleads with his hands on my shoulders, "you've got to do something! The robot will be here in just a matter of minutes. He is ruining our city! If you don't do something, we will all be crushed! Please, Nate, please!"

"Me? Why me?" I ask, wondering why this powerful and strong leader would want my help. Isn't *he* the one who is supposed to protect *us?*

The mayor bends down close and looks me in the eye. "Why because you're Nate Rocks, of course! Now go! There is no time to waste."

I look around to a sea of terrified eyes staring at me. Yes, I've got to do something. Everyone here is depending on me. I run up the basement steps and out of the building. Debris is flying all around as the robot turns the corner, taking out the movie theater with a single swipe of its mechanical arm. He is still several blocks away from City Hall, but moving closer by the second. The sound of his steps combined with the destruction around me is deafening.

Halfway down the street I spot it...the old train station that's been closed for years. The city has been working to restore it into some kind of historical landmark. The front has been covered with metal scaffolding for months now. That's it! I race down the street, toward the train station and the robot, as fast as I can possibly run. I have to time everything perfectly or my plan will fail.

As I reach the train station, I grab hold of the metal ladder and hoist myself up to the first landing on the scaffolding. Not high enough. I jump up to grab on to the next set of ladders and proceed to climb at a rapid pace until I am on the roof of the building. The robot is just steps away. I crouch behind a metal beam to stay out of sight. As the robot approaches, I leap from the roof onto the giant machine's shoulder, just as he knocks the train station to the ground. I swiftly slide to the back of the robot, out of his line of vision, and lower myself carefully down until I find the square door. *Just as I suspected!* I open the door to the control panel on his back. Different colored wires hum as they power the robot's every move. With all my strength, I pull the wires, detaching them from the monster. I hold tight as he collapses to the ground in defeat just steps away from City Hall. Silence suddenly fills the air around me, but not for long.

Everyone comes running out of the building

cheering. The mayor swings me through the air as the crowd chants:

"Nate!"

"Nate!"

"Nate!"

"Nathan! Are you listening?"

"Huh?" I look up to see Mom standing over my shoulder.

"Nathan, why are you drawing pictures all over that permission form? You know you have to return that to school today!" Mom takes the slip of paper out of my hands. "Honestly, Nathan, now where am I supposed to sign? You've drawn robots everywhere. Don't you want to go on this trip?"

Of course I want to go! One of the perks of moving up to fifth grade is the trip in the spring to New York City. Who wouldn't want to go? Actually, now that I think about it, I kind of remember my older sister, Abby, complaining that she didn't want to go back when she was in fifth grade...something about not being able to bring her curling iron. I guess she didn't want anyone to see her without her hair done. Girls! Although, I can't say I really blame her there. I shudder just thinking about it. Oooh...maybe that annoying classmate of mine, Lisa Crane, won't want to go either. All she is going to do anyway is act like she knows everything about everything. That's what she does. I have to admit; it was kind of nice getting away from her over the summer when I went to overnight camp with my best friend, Tommy. But now that we're back, and school has started up again, I feel like Lisa is everywhere I turn.

As for me, there is no doubt in my mind that I want to go on this trip. Are you kidding? We'll get to spend two whole nights in a fancy hotel, walk around New York City, and eat all our meals in restaurants. If you count the meals we'll eat on the way there and back, that's nine meals cooked by someone other than Mom. Mom's cooking is, well, I'm not going to lie. It's not even the tiniest bit good. Nine meals of non-mom cooking is worth it...even if Lisa Crane does wind up going on the trip. Besides, Tommy and my other good friend, Sam, for sure will go also. It's kind of a no-brainer, well except that I'll miss my puppy, Bobino, but I know Dad will take care of him and protect him from Abby. Abby *claims* she doesn't like dogs all of a sudden. But she's just jealous that Mom and Dad let me keep him even though she'd been asking for a dog for years. She *says* Bobino smells and keeps getting into her stuff. What does she know? Bobino is the best puppy ever. I even gave him an extra treat when he ate Abby's new shoes. Payback for everything she did to me at camp. Let's just call it even now.

"Nathan, the form has an area to mark off for me to be a chaperone on the trip," Mom says, looking at me with that weird, happy expression she gets when she wants to do something. "Would you like me to go?"

I go into perma-grin mode as I force a smile. "Oh...uh...sure," I somehow manage to say. My brain on the other hand screams, "NO! PLEASE, OH PLEASE, NO! ANYTHING EXCEPT THAT!"

Mom beams. "Well, let me call Marge and see if she can go also. Wouldn't that be just so much fun?"

Marge? Marge *Crane?* As in *Lisa Crane's* mother? I know Marge is Mom's best friend and all, but really? If Mrs. Crane goes, Mom will make Lisa and I do everything together. *Everything.* I absolutely cannot let that happen. Yet I just keep nodding, perma-grin still in place, as I say, "Yeah...uh...fun."

"Oh sugar!" Mom says, looking at the form again. "I can't go that weekend, and neither can Marge. Her sister's best friend's aunt's daughter is getting married the weekend after that. She's a real nice girl. She goes to the local university, and her husband-to-be is there also. He's studying to be some sort of chemical researcher or something. I don't really get it, but Marge says he's always got his nose in a book. Anyway, Marge promised to help prepare some of the food for the party since her sister's best friend's uncle just lost his job, and they can't afford a big fancy wedding. I promised to help also, so I won't be able to go after all."

First of all, Mom lost me with that story after the first three words, but it's kind of impressive that she was able to remember all that. Second of all, phew.

"Oh," I say, trying to find the perfect balance between disappointment and pure excitement, leaning slightly on the disappointment side for Mom's benefit.

"I know you're sad, Nathan. I'm sorry. Maybe Dad

can go with you instead?"

"I guess," I reply, still working on the right tone. I'd rather have neither of my parents come along, but given the choice; I'd pick Dad hands down.

"Anyway, cheer up. There's a lot to look forward to this school year. You've got the big Halloween party at school next month, the trip to New York City in the spring, and...someone I know has a birthday this weekend."

It's true. I'm turning eleven on Sunday. My party is on Saturday, and I cannot wait! Usually, Mom insists on throwing parties at our house, while all the other kids have parties outside of their homes at cool places like the movie theater or the mini golf place. I've been begging to have a party outside of my house for years, but Mom always says no, claiming no one throws better parties than she does. She plans all these corny games that I guess were kind of fun when I was six, like pin the tail on the donkey and red light/green light. Once I hit ten they started getting a little embarrassing. Last year our red light/green light game kind of got a little wild, and my friend Eli knocked over Mom's favorite lamp. It smashed into a million pieces. Well not really, but it was more pieces than Dad could easily glue back together, and the lamp had to be thrown away.

Mom was really upset. It was some sort of family treasure or something, which I thought was pretty cool, because who knew there were treasures in the Rockledge family. But then I started thinking; why would you put something so valuable in a room where fifteen ten year olds would be running around? If you ask me, it seemed like a pretty irresponsible thing for a treasure holder to do.

This year, Mom suggested I have my party outside of the house. I'll have to remember to thank Eli. Anyway, I chose laser tag. For some reason that I am not about to question, Mom agreed, which is totally bizarre because she has this weird obsession about me not doing anything that involves any kind of weapon whatsoever. I'm not even allowed to carry a sword made out of cardboard and tin foil on Halloween! My guess is that she has no clue laser tag actually involves shooting each other with laser guns in the dark. I'm not about to tell her either since my party is just days away.

Yup, a laser gun birthday, a big Halloween party at school next month, a trip to New York City in the spring...what can I say? Fifth grade is totally going to rock!

Chapter 2

"Nathan! Are you ready? We're going to be late!"

"Coming!" I run down the steps, two at a time, with Bobino at my heels. Mom, Dad, and Abby are all waiting at the door for me.

"Do I really have to go?" Abby whines.

"Yes, Abby, it's your brother's birthday."

"His birthday is tomorrow," she replies, as if I am not even in the room.

"But his party is today, and you're going," Mom says, sounding more annoyed with every word.

"It's fine with me," I say. "She doesn't need to come." Honestly, if Abby wants to stay home let her. In fact, I'd rather she did stay home. At the party, she's just going to stand in a corner either sulking or texting— actually, probably both. What's the point of her being there anyway?

"You see?" Abby says. "Nathan doesn't care if I'm there."

"We're a family," Mom says in that *I'm about to lose my patience tone,* "and we are going to celebrate Nathan's birthday together...as a family. Now get your coat, Abby." Mom clears her throat before going back to her normal happy voice. "Bill, can you grab the cake? I made your favorite, Nathan,

8

chocolate with vanilla frosting."

Chocolate with vanilla frosting is my favorite... when it comes from the bakery. Oh well, it's the thought that counts. Luckily, most of my friends have been to enough of my birthday parties to know to stay away from Mom's cake.

"Ooh," Dad says, bringing the cake in from the kitchen, "that's my favorite, too, Nathan. Hey, did I ever tell you about the time Uncle Robert and I tried to bake a cake for Grandma for her birthday?"

I look at Dad. "You mean the time you put the cake in the oven and then went outside to play?"

Dad gets that familiar glazed look in his eyes he gets whenever traveling down memory lane. "Yup. We forgot all about the cake. Grandma smelled smoke from upstairs and called the fire department. She was not happy." Dad snaps out of his mini-trance. "Anyway, lucky for us, Mom here never lets that happen. I sure did marry a gourmet cook."

"Yeah," I say, trying to sound convincing. "Uh, shouldn't we get going?" It's my first out of the house birthday party. I want to actually get *out of the house* before Mom changes her mind.

"Fine!" Abby complains, coming back into the room with her coat. "But don't expect me to play laser tag with Nathan's weird friends. And *don't* take any pictures of me. The last thing I want is to be seen with a bunch of ten-year-olds."

"Um, most of my friends are eleven, and I'll be turning eleven tomorrow, remember?"

"Whatever," Abby says. Bobino jumps up on her as she buttons her jacket. "Ugh!" she yells, pushing him back. "Get this mangy mutt off of me."

"He just wants you to pet him. Why can't you be nice to him?" I pick up Bobino and put him behind the gate in the kitchen.

"All right, you two. Let's go," Dad says.

"Just pretend like you don't know me when we get there," Abby whispers, as we walk out the door.

Trust me, that won't be a problem.

The parking lot for the laser tag place is jammed-packed. Actually, it's a bowling/arcade/laser tag place, but all I really care about is the laser tag part. We're a little early, so I don't see any of my friends yet.

I wanted to have an all boys' party, but Mom insisted I invite Lisa Crane. I was so worried Mom would change her mind about having the party out of the house, that I pretty much agreed to everything she asked, including inviting Lisa. Now that I see Lisa walking towards me, I'm beginning to have second thoughts.

"Hi, Nathan," she shrills.

"Hi, Lisa," I mumble under my breath. Oh where are Tommy and Sam? I'll take *anyone* for that matter; I just need *someone* to rescue me away from Lisa.

"Hi, Lisa. I'm so glad you could make it," Mom says, joining us.

"Hi, Mrs. Rockledge," Lisa replies.

"Did Nathan tell you how excited he is for the party today?" Mom asks. "He had so much trouble falling asleep. I thought I was going to have to rub his back and sing to him like I used to when he was little. Remember, Nathan? I'd give you a nice warm bath and then wrap you in your bunny towel and ..."

Well, maybe not *anyone*. "O-okay, Mom," I say, trying to get her to stop. "Oh look, Tommy and Sam are here. I'll be right back." I run off with no real intention of returning to Lisa and Mom.

"Nathan," Tommy yells, "this is so cool! How'd you get your mom to agree to this?"

"Shh." I put my finger up to my lips. "I have no idea, but let's not give her any reason to think she *shouldn't* have agreed to it, you know what I'm saying?"

The rest of my friends arrive in the next few minutes. We hang out in the lobby goofing around as Mom talks to the person behind the counter.

Feedback and static from an intercom system suddenly fills the room. "Rockledge party: Please report to the laser tag area," the voice says over the crackling sound.

"That's us," Mom calls, coming towards me again. "Is everyone here, Nathan?"

I scan my friends...six boys and Lisa. Abby, as predicted, is leaning up against the wall in the corner, texting.

"I think so," I say, as we all walk toward the back of the room where the big LASER TAG sign is displayed.

"The Rockledge party is here," Dad announces to a teenage girl standing behind a counter as if we are celebrities or something. The girl seems to be completely uninterested as we crowd around her.

"Okay," she says, cracking her gum in between words. "You got fifteen minutes in this round." She pulls out a pile of vests and hands out one to each person. As we put them on, she pulls out a laser gun. "You can shoot your opponent in either the front or back of the vest. Once you are hit—"

"Um, excuse me," Mom interrupts, pushing her way to the front. "Did you say *shoot?*"

"Uh-huh," the girl says, blowing a large bubble with her gum before snapping it back into her mouth.

Oh no! I look at Tommy and cringe.

"No, no," Mom continues. "I think there's been a mistake. We're here for a game of tag. You know, you run around until someone yells, *You're it?* We didn't ask for anything with guns."

The girl looks at Mom as if she is crazy. Maybe not letting Mom know exactly what laser tag meant ahead of time wasn't the best decision after all. I decide I need to say something, since the girl looks like her head might explode from trying to understand what Mom has just said.

"They're not guns, Mom," I say, with my best innocent looking face, "they're *lasers.*" I pick up one of the non-gun lasers to show her. "See? They are just like giant flashlights. A light beam comes out of it, and if someone *happens* to run *in front* of the light, then they get tagged. Just like in regular tag, except we aren't using our hands, we're using laser gu—er—flashlights. Laser flashlights. Isn't that right?" I ask the girl, nodding slowly at her. *Please agree,* I plead using my eyes and nodding head. *Please. Agree.*

She raises one eyebrow at me, "Sure, kid. Whatever," she responds.

"See, Mom? No guns or shooting going on here. Just a nice, fun game of tag with flashlights."

"I don't know," Mom begins. "Bill, what do you think? You know I hate anything violent, and I don't want these kids going home telling their parents we gave them guns to shoot. I won't be able to show my face around town ever again."

"Not guns, Mom, *flashlights.* Remember? Dad...a little help, please?" I look at my dad. Come on, Dad. You were a kid once. Somewhere in there I know you've got a story about you and Uncle Robert pretending to have laser guns as kids. Right? Please?

"Oh, Claudia," my dad *finally* says, "I think playing tag with flashlights sounds fun. I think it will be just fine. After all, it is Nathan's birthday."

I breathe a sigh of relief. I knew I could count on him.

Mom looks at me first and then at the girl behind the counter. "Oh, okay, I suppose flashlight tag does sound kind of fun."

The girl behind the counter rolls her eyes and continues, "As I was saying, you take your gun—"

"Flashlight," I remind her.

"... and try to shoot—" she says.

"Tag," I interrupt again, "you try to *tag.*"

The girl glares at me and cracks her gum once more, only louder this time. She throws a pile of laser guns on the counter. "Here's your stuff. You've got fifteen minutes." She starts to walk away and then comes back, reaching under the counter for some forms and pencils. "Oh and write your name on these scorecards. You *are* allowed to use pencils, aren't you?" she asks, looking at me.

"Yes," I mumble, gathering up my equipment.

Chapter 3

"Hey, Abby," Lisa says loudly, walking towards my sister. Apparently she found herself a new wall to lean against to continue texting and sulking. "Don't you want to play?"

"Nah," Abby replies, without even looking up.

"Aw, come on. We can show these boys how it's done. Don't forget, I've got pretty good aim."

Ugh, please don't bring that up again. Not at my party!

Lisa continues, "Remember at your barbecue over the summer when Nathan and I were playing horseshoes? He missed every shot." Lisa turns around and stares right at me.

Yup, she's bringing it up. Great. Just great.

"Isn't that right, Nathan?" Lisa asks, even louder now. My friends all stop getting their equipment together and look up.

"Let's go already," I say to the others, trying to divert the conversation. "The clock's ticking. I'm going in." I take a step toward the door, but Lisa keeps right on talking.

"And then when it was my turn to throw that horseshoe...clink! Perfect shot. Remember, Nathan? Of course, I would have gotten the second one too, but you just refused to get out of the way, and my horseshoe smacked you right in the face. I'm not saying you deserved that black eye, Nathan, but really, why *were* you standing so close to me?" Lisa smiles and bats her eyelashes. I can feel my face getting hot and bright red.

"What?" I stammer, looking around at my friends who are now all standing around us. "That's not at all what happened."

Abby pushes her way through my circle of friends. "Actually, Nathan, that's exactly what happened." She grabs a vest and laser gun and walks through the door into the laser tag arena.

"Nathan, you couldn't hit a target if it were two feet in front of you. This is going to be a breeze," Lisa adds and follows Abby into the room, letting the door slam shut behind her.

I look at my friends and mumble once more, "That's not how it happened." Some party this is turning out to be. I head over to the counter.

"Don't forget to write your name on your scorecards," the girl behind the desk utters without looking up.

Tommy puts his arm around my shoulder. "Don't worry about Lisa, Nathan. She's just trying to rile you up. Shake it off. We're going to have a blast."

"Yeah," Sam says. "Nobody listens to Lisa anyway. Besides, we all know she's only here because your mom made you invite her. Come on; let's go in before the time runs out. This is going to be so much fun. Begin *Operation Destroy Lisa*. Right fellas?"

"Yeah!" I agree. "Oh and Abby, too! Don't forget

Abby. This is my party, and I'm not going to let a bunch of annoying girls ruin it for me!" We all high-five each other as we walk through the door.

I'm now completely pumped up and ready. Finally, we get to play laser tag. I honestly have no idea what to expect, thanks to Mom's whole non-weapon rule, but who cares. The room is pitch black and quiet, except for the sound of our footsteps. As my eyes start to adjust slightly, I can see what looks like some sort of barriers—maybe rocks or barrels—along with platforms and ladders.

Tommy and Sam have disappeared. I guess they've already gone into hiding. I should do that myself. Before I can make my way behind a barrel, I see a shadow move out of the corner of my eye. I reach for my gun and back up slowly. One thing I do know about laser tag is that you don't want to make any sudden moves.

"Hey, watch it!" the unfamiliar voice says quietly, yet firmly.

"Tommy?" I slowly turn around, even though I know for a fact the voice is *not* Tommy's. In fact, I'm pretty sure that voice doesn't belong to anyone I invited to my party. That girl at the desk didn't say there would be other people in here.

"Tommy who? Is he part of the team?" the voice whispers.

"I guess," I say, a bit confused. This must be our party against another birthday party. I should probably get out of the way before this guy figures out I'm on the other team and starts shooting at me. I start to tiptoe away.

"Wait...I didn't realize it was you," he says. "Don't go, Nate! We need your help!"

A flash of light goes off in the distance. The sound of an explosion quickly follows. Wow, these laser guns really have some great sound effects. I've been missing out. I carefully move back closer to the mystery person. "How do you know my name?" I question. I guess I'm supposed to be on this guy's team after all.

My eyes are now getting used to the dark, and I notice that the person is wearing a camouflage helmet. As a matter of fact, my head feels a bit heavier then it did earlier. I put my hand on my head to feel my own helmet. I look down and notice I'm wearing a matching camouflage outfit as well as heavy combat boots.

"Uh...what's going on?" I hesitantly ask.

"It's the enemy. They've captured our general, and we've got to get him out before they realize he's carrying classified information that could be used against us. You've got to help him, Nate, please!"

"Classified information? We're not in the laser tag place anymore are we," I say more as a statement rather than a question.

"Laser tag? What are you talking about? This is no game, Nate. This is serious, and we need your help! *Operation Birthday Bash* is in full swing."

"Operation Birthday Bash?"

"Yeah," the guy explains, "that's code for we need to save the General. You're the only one who can do it, Nate."

"Me? Why me?" I ask.

"Why because you're Nate Rocks, of course! Look, they've got him over there in that cave," he says, pointing to a large stone mountain.

The man hands me his binoculars. In the distance, I can see the cave. There is a small opening to it, where two heavily armed, burly men are stationed. There's no way I can possibly get in there without those guards noticing, and they're huge. They'll crush me flatter than the pancakes Dad makes on Christmas morning.

"Hurry, Nate, we don't have much time. The enemy line is getting closer. We've got to get our general out before they all reach the cave, or we won't have any chance of rescuing him."

I take another look at the two men guarding the entrance of the cave. There has to be a different way. I try to get a bearing of my surroundings. There is a second, larger mountain directly next to us. It's risky, but it just might work.

"Wait here," I instruct.

I begin to scale the closest mountain as quickly and quietly as I possibly can. As I approach the top, I close my eyes and take a deep breath. *You can do this, Nate.* I swing my arms and use all my energy to leap to the next mountain. My feet barely reach the edge. As I steady myself, I notice I can see the back of the cave where the General is being held prisoner. As I suspected, there is no opening and no guards around the back. If I can create an opening with my laser, the General can escape. I survey the back of the cave once more before raising my laser gun up to my eye level. One false shot and the entire mountain will crumble, crushing the General. My hands begin to shake as I hear Lisa's last words to me: *You couldn't hit a target if it were two feet in front of you.* Calm yourself, Nate, you can do this. I take a second deep breath, steady my weapon, aim, and...fire. A green light beam escapes from my gun and heads in the direction of the cave. It makes direct contact, creating the perfect opening for the General to escape. The noise from the laser hitting the back of the cave blends in perfectly with the sound of the enemy fighting in the distance. The two guards in the front do not seem the least bit alarmed.

I race across the mountain range, meeting the General as he stumbles out.

"General, are you okay?" I ask, taking his hand and leading him down the back of the mountain. An army tank is there to meet us.

"Nate," the General says, shaking my hand. "You have saved our country from great danger! How can I ever thank you?"

I take his arm and guide him into the tanker. "Oh it was nothing," I respond.

The General looks at me. "I've never seen anyone with such good aim. You are one brave soldier. In fact, I think you may be one of the bravest soldiers I've ever met. Do you hear me, kid?"

"Kid?"

"Hey, kid! I said write your name, not doodle a scene out of Armageddon. Geez." The girl behind the laser tag counter crumples up the slip and hands me another one. "Name," she repeats. "Do you think you can handle that, soldier?"

"Yeah," I reply smiling. "I think I can."

Chapter 4

"But I thought everything was all set. Isn't that why our parents had to sign that permission form and pay the deposit?" I ask Tommy at recess.

The whole reason I was looking forward to fifth grade was for the New York City trip. It was a major selling point—not that I had a choice as to whether or not to attend fifth grade, but still. Of course there are other perks that come along with being in fifth grade. For example, we no longer are subjected to those awful kickball games that we used to have to play at recess. Oh, they were the worst! Four years of ruined recesses thanks to being forced to play that horrid game. Thank goodness that's over. I guess fifth graders think they're too cool to hang out with the lower grades now. So instead, we sort of all just scatter into small groups and do, well, whatever. Sometimes Tommy tries to get me to play basketball with him. It's not my favorite, but it's better than kickball. The best is when the teachers bring out the baseball equipment and let us play on the field that's across from the playground. I do love baseball. I especially love watching baseball when the Phillies are playing. They're my favorite team. Dad says he might be able to get some tickets to see them play this spring. That would be awesome. Anyway, whenever the teachers let us play baseball at recess, I always have a good time. Today, however, we're just hanging out, talking about the trip that might not actually happen.

"That form was just to see how many kids had permission to go on the trip. Nothing is final until the fundraising is finished," Tommy explains.

"What do you mean?" I ask.

"Well, it's expensive to take a bunch of kids to New York City. The school helps pay for some of it, but then we have to raise the rest of the money ourselves. Didn't you know that?"

I guess I never thought of it like that before. I just assumed the money part was taken care of. I don't remember Abby having to do any fundraising. I'll bet her class used up all the money on their trip, and that's why there's none left for my class. Figures.

"Hey, Nathan! Cool party on Saturday!" Sam says, joining Tommy and me.

It's a good thing all the fifth graders have recess and lunch together; otherwise I'd never get to see Sam during the school day. We live in the same neighborhood, but since his mom won't let him cross the street by himself, he's at a different bus stop. I had hoped that this year, since he is now in fifth grade, his mom might have changed her mind about the no crossing the street rule, but no such luck. So because he's at a different stop, he's also on a completely different bus from Tommy and me. I wonder how old Sam needs to be before his mom lets him cross the street by himself? I really don't understand how our parents come up with some of these rules.

"Thanks, Sam," I respond. "I thought so, too."

The party actually was pretty amazing. Tommy, Sam, and I decided to be a team once we finally got into the laser tag room. There were strobe lights going off in each corner, and the music was pretty loud. Once I got used to it all, however, I really was able to get my game on. I hid behind a rock, while Tommy climbed to the platform, manning the pretend rooftop. Sam stayed underneath and hid behind some old barrels. At the top of our most wanted list: Abby and Lisa. Turned out none of us had very good aim, but it actually worked to our advantage. Not only did we hit Abby and Lisa, we also managed to unintentionally hit just about everyone else in the room as well, including each other. Our scores weren't the best, but it didn't matter, we had fun and that's what counted the most. Even Lisa's gloating that she scored higher than me didn't break my good mood. After we were done with our game, we had pizza and then a second round of laser tag. My aim still stunk, but I definitely did better. Lucky for us, we only had a few minutes for cake at the end, so Mom didn't notice that no one really even ate it. I think she had a pretty good time, too, and she didn't have to worry about any other Rockledge treasures getting ruined.

"So what are you guys talking about?" Sam asks.

"The school trip to New York City," Tommy replies.

"You mean *the maybe if we can actually raise*

enough money to go on the school trip to New York City," I sulk.

"Stop being so negative, Nathan," Tommy says. "When was the last time a fifth grade class missed the trip to New York City?"

"Um...I don't know," I answer.

"That's because it's never happened," Tommy says. "The school always makes sure the fifth graders get to go. Think about it. They wouldn't get us all excited and stuff just to say: *Sorry kids, you have a loser class this year, and we're not sending you.* Right?"

"Make sense to me," Sam agrees. "I think you're worried about nothing, Nathan."

"Besides, the trip isn't until the spring. That's a lot of time for us to come up with the money, and there are lots of things we can do to make money," Tommy says.

"Like what?" I ask. If making money were so easy, why is Dad always complaining he doesn't make enough of it?

"Well," Tommy begins, "we could uh...um ..."

"Ooh," Sam says, "maybe we could ask your parents to pay us to walk Bobino."

"I don't think so," I say. "That's one of my chores. If I don't walk him, Mom says she'll find another home for him. She's not going to start paying for something I do for free."

"Well, what about other dogs? We could start a dog walking business."

"Are there any other dogs in the neighborhood?" Tommy asks.

"Just Snowflake across the street," I reply. "You know, that Saint Bernard? I've seen Mr. Landon try to walk him. It doesn't exactly look easy, and he's a pretty big guy. I'm not sure even the three of us together could handle that dog."

"Nathan," Sam says, "didn't you say your sister always seems to have extra money?"

"You want me to ask Abby for money for the trip?" I ask, confused because I'm pretty sure she won't give me a penny. In fact, I'm absolutely one hundred percent sure she won't give me even a quarter of a penny.

"No, I was just wondering how it is that she gets her money."

"Babysitting, mostly. Can you believe people actually trust her with their kids? Don't they know that as soon as they walk out the door all Abby does is text her friends? I feel sorry for those poor kids. All she has to do is play games with them, I mean how hard is that?"

"Exactly!" Tommy exclaims.

"Exactly what?" I ask. I sure wish my friends would stop saying stuff that doesn't make any sense.

"Great idea, Tommy!" Sam agrees.

"What's a great idea?" I question, getting annoyed. "Could somebody please explain this great idea to me?"

Tommy and Sam both look at me and smile. "Babysitting!" they say together.

"Babysitting? I don't know anything about babysitting!"

"Nathan, you just said it yourself. All we have to do is play games with kids! How hard can that be? Getting paid to play games? Sounds like a dream job. You want to go on this trip don't you?" asks Tommy.

"Yeah."

"We can go around to the neighbors and ask them if they need us to watch their kids afterschool or on the weekends," Sam suggests. "Hey, Tommy, do you think your mom will let us babysit your little brother?"

"Maybe," Tommy responds. "I know she was just saying to my dad the other day that she wanted to go out this weekend. Usually my grandma comes over, but I guess I could ask my mom if we could do it instead."

"After we watch your brother, we can say we're *experienced*. That's bound to get us more jobs. We'll be on our way to New York City in no time!" Sam says excitedly.

"Whatcha boys talking about?"

I turn around to see Lisa standing behind me.

"Nothing," I answer, shaking my head at Tommy and Sam to let them know not to say a word. The last thing I need is for Lisa Crane to get involved in our moneymaking plans.

"Whatever," Lisa snaps, rolling her eyes. "I was just coming over to tell you that Mrs. Cogin wants us to come inside a little early so we can have some extra time today to review for our math test. It seems we all have to suffer just because *some* of us aren't doing so well in math these days." Lisa glares at me before marching off.

"Well *some* of us have a life outside of school," I yell at her back.

"Boy she really has it out for you, doesn't she?" Sam remarks.

"Whatever," I say. "Come on, Tommy. Let's head in. See you later, Sam."

"See you guys," Sam replies. "Hey, Tommy, don't forget to ask your mom, okay?"

"Got it," Tommy says.

Chapter 5

"Babysitting! What do you know about babysitting?" Abby asks, as we eat our dinner. Apparently Mom is experimenting with possible Thanksgiving type dishes, because tonight's dinner consists of rubbery turkey, cold gravy with unidentifiable things floating in it, and what I think is supposed to be mashed potatoes, but looks more like that lumpy glue we used in art class today. Luckily, the carrots look relatively harmless. But you never can be too sure with Mom's cooking.

"What's to know? It's Tommy's little brother. All we have to do is play with him for two hours while Tommy's parents go to some meeting tonight."

After several unsuccessful attempts, I stab a piece of my meat with my fork. I wonder how far it would bounce if I were to fling it against the wall. I decide that's probably not the best idea and pretend to take a bite. Luckily, Tommy's mom always has great snacks at her house. Good thing, too, seeing as though I will be starving later.

"Babysitting, huh? Hey, Nathan, did I ever tell you about the time Grandmom let Uncle Robert babysit me for the first time?" Dad asks.

"You mean the time Uncle Robert let you eat an entire gallon of ice cream for dinner?"

"Yeah," Dad says in his weird memory voice. "I was so sick, I had to stay home from school the next day. Grandmom didn't let Uncle Robert babysit me again for a whole year." Dad snaps back into reality and says, "Well, I'm sure you boys know better than that. Right, Nathan?"

"Uh, yeah," I say, getting up. I pick up my plate and head over to the sink. "Anyway, I've got to get over to Tommy's house. I don't want to be late."

"But, Nathan, you've barely eaten your dinner!" Mom says, taking my plate right out of my hands before I can dump it in the sink.

"Oh, I'll just grab something at Tommy's place. Mrs. Jensen always makes extra."

"Well, I'll just wrap this up for your lunch tomorrow, then. You know what they say... Thanksgiving food always tastes best the next day."

"Um, thanks," I say, grabbing my jacket off the hook by the door. *"I sure hope so,"* I say to myself.

"What's that, Nathan?" Mom asks, as she opens the door.

I did say that silently, didn't I? "Oh nothing, Mom, just saying goodbye. See you in a few hours."

"Okay. We're home if you need anything. I can always send Abby over."

Abby sticks her tongue out at me as I look over to her. "Thanks, but I'm sure we'll be fine. See ya."

Tommy's little brother, Andy, is already in his

pajamas by the time I get to Tommy's house. Sam is already there as well.

"Now you sure you boys will be okay?" Mrs. Jensen asks, looking a bit nervous.

"We've got this, Mom, don't worry," Tommy confidently states.

Mrs. Jensen points to a piece of paper on the table. "I've got all the phone numbers you'll need right here: my cell number, Dad's cell, the doctor, the hospital, 9-1-1, and the Rockledge's." She looks at me and continues, "Nathan, your mom said you can call if you need anything, okay?"

Mr. Jensen puts his hand on Mrs. Jensen's shoulder and says, "I'm guessing Nathan knows his own phone number. Isn't that right, son?"

"Yes, sir," I respond.

He pulls Mrs. Jensen towards the door. "We should get going before we're late. The boys will be just fine."

"Okay, okay. Bye, boys. Don't forget, if you need anything ..."

"We know, Mom, the phone numbers are on the paper."

Mom smiles. "Be good, Andy. Don't forget, bed in a half-hour," she says and walks out the door.

"Finally," Tommy says with a big grin on his face. "I thought they'd never leave!"

"So what should we do?" I ask. To be honest, I hadn't really planned anything past the getting Tommy's mom to agree to let us babysit part.

"Well...we could go hangout in my tree house or something," Tommy says, looking at Sam and me.

"But, aren't we supposed to be watching your little brother?" Sam asks.

"Yeah, tree house! I want to hang out in the tree house!" Andy yells.

"You're not allowed in my tree house, remember? How about a game? Do you want to play a game, Andy?" Tommy asks.

"Yeah, a game, a game, a game," he repeats.

"I know! We can play hide and seek!" Sam blurts out.

Hide and seek? That's for babies.

"Hide and seek! Hide and seek! Hide and seek!" Andy screams.

"I think he wants to play hide and seek," I mumble.

"Oh, all right," Tommy says, "one game of hide and seek, and then it's time for you to get ready for bed."

"Me hide first," Andy says.

Sam shrugs. "Okay."

"You count," Andy orders.

The three of us—Tommy, Sam, and I—all turn to face the wall in the living room, and we start counting, "1-2-3-4-"

"Slower!" Andy yells.

We start over. "1...2...3...4 ..." We hear all kinds of noises: little feet running through rooms and sounds of banging doors from the closets. Finally, we hear Andy go into the laundry room at the back of the house. We finish counting to 25.

"Ready or not, here we come!" Tommy yells. He motions toward the door to the room we heard Andy go through, and we all nod. Poor kid. One of these days he'll figure out how to hide quietly and in a not so obvious place.

"Wait," Sam says. "He'll be disappointed if we find him right away."

We all nod. "Hey, how about a quick game of Space Shooters?" Tommy asks, grabbing the video game controller from on top of the television.

"Sure," we all agree.

Since Tommy only has two controllers, I decide to let Tommy and Sam play. "Hey guys, do you mind if I grab a snack while you're playing? I didn't have dinner," I say.

"Sure," Tommy responds without looking up.

I head into the kitchen where I see a bowl of popcorn sitting out on the table. *Perfect.* I grab a handful and sit down. The paper with all the phone numbers is right in front of me. I don't know why, but I start reading down the list. My phone number is listed last. I chuckle, thinking about how funny it is that Mrs. Jensen would think a fifth-grader wouldn't know his own phone number. The funny part though, is that Mrs. Jensen wrote the wrong number down. I pick up the pencil so I can cross out the five and write in a seven instead.

I look up as I hear the side door to the kitchen open up.

"Nate! Thank goodness. I was hoping you'd be here!"

A uniformed police officer walks through the door and stands in front of me. Uh-oh.

"What'd I do?" I stammer. "I...uh...I mean... whatever it is, I swear I didn't do it." I push myself up and away from the table, backing up into the refrigerator.

"Huh? No. We need your help, Nate. One of the neighbors just called to report that a little boy down the street has gone missing! You've got to help us find him!"

"But how can I help?" I ask.

"Word on the street is that Nate Rocks is an expert babysitter."

"Well, really I just started ..."

"Oh stop being so humble, Nate. Now please, we don't have much time! We've got to find this little boy, and we've got to find him now!"

I follow the policeman as he runs back out the door. He's walking up the street yelling, "Johnny! Come on out, Johnny!"

A young woman comes running down the street toward me. She is crying hysterically. "Nate, please! You have to find my Johnny! I thought he was playing on the patio, but now I can't find him! It is starting to get dark, and he's afraid of the dark. Pleeeaaasseee!"

"Nate," the police officer says, "we're depending on you."

Without hesitation I start running down the street through people's yards yelling, "Johnny, Johnny!" I've got to find him. Where could he be? I look around. Tommy's house has completely disappeared. In fact, this isn't even his neighborhood! It's too bad, because whenever I need a place to go to think and figure things out, I go over to Tommy's tree house; either that or I just climb a tree. There's something about being up high and hanging out in the trees. In fact, if I were going to hide somewhere, I'd head straight up the nearest tr—That's it! I run through each backyard, looking up to the trees. When I get to the last house on the street, I stop short. I lean up against its back wall as I try to catch my breath. Darn, I was so sure he'd be hanging out in a tree or something. I shake my head and look at the ground.

Suddenly, I hear a small whimper coming from the side of the house. As I make my way over, I notice a tree house above me. I climb the ladder with a burst of energy. Sure enough, a young boy is sitting on the floor, crying.

"Johnny?" I ask.

He nods.

"Come on," I say, "I'll help you down."

As we make our way down the ladder, his mom and the police officer are running toward us. His mom scoops up the young boy in her arms.

"Thank you, Nate! Thank you!" she cries, hugging me while she holds her son.

A man, who appears to be the boy's father, runs to where we are standing and takes the boy from the woman, giving him a big hug. He then looks at me and asks, "So tell me, where did you find him, Nate? Nate?"

"Are you listening? I said: We need to find him, Nathan!"

"Huh?" I look up to see Tommy and Sam looking at me frantically.

"Stop drawing all over my Mom's paper. We need your help. We lost track of time, and now we can't find Andy anywhere," Tommy explains.

"I think I might know exactly where he is," I say, putting down the pencil.

Chapter 6

"I'm telling you, Nathan, he didn't go outside! I would have heard him," Tommy says in a panicked tone as he follows me toward the door in the laundry room, which leads to the backyard. "The back door creaks so loudly that the next door neighbors can hear it. Mom says it's way better than any fancy alarm system."

"What about the front door or the side door? We had our eyes closed, remember? Andy could have gotten out that way," Sam states.

"Nah, he can't reach the locks on those doors. They're too high up. Mom keeps asking Dad to put one like that on the back door, too, but Dad still hasn't gotten around to it. I guess he figures since it creaks so much and all. There's no way Andy got outside without us hearing that door open. Anyway, I could have sworn he was hiding behind the washer. He always hides in the laundry room. Maybe we should look in the dryer again."

"We checked there three times already," Sam says.

I ignore my friends and keep walking towards the door. "Really, just trust me," I say.

"I think we should try the basement again," Sam offers, apparently having no trust in me after all. I don't know why I even bother sometimes.

"No, we searched down there already," Tommy says. "Besides, Andy's afraid to go down there by himself. I'm guessing it's because I keep telling him about the monster who lives under the steps."

"What monster?" Sam asks.

I stop walking and look at Sam in disbelief. Did he really just say *what monster?* I get that Andy might believe there is a monster living under the steps, but Sam?

"There is no monster," I tell him. "Tommy just wanted to make sure Andy stayed away from the castle he made out of Legos. Isn't that right, Tommy?"

"Well, I did hear a noise once when I was down there," Tommy responds, shrugging his shoulders.

"Really? Do you think it was the monster?" Sam asks.

"There is no monster!" I yell, shaking my head. "Now can we get back to looking for Andy? That video game the two of you were playing was pretty loud. I could hear it all the way in the kitchen. The noise from that could have easily drowned out the sound of the back door opening."

Tommy nods, nearly in tears. "My parents are never going to let me do anything again...ever. I'm going to be grounded for the rest of my life. I won't even be able to take those weird dance classes when I get older that my grandparents take at their senior center because I'll still be grounded! We've got to find him!" Tommy cups his hands around his mouth and starts yelling, "Andy! This isn't funny!

You need to come out! Now!"

"Don't worry," I say, grabbing a flashlight off the laundry room shelf and pushing the back door open. Sure enough, the door creaks loudly. "Wow, you weren't kidding."

"Told you," Tommy says. "Do you really think he went outside?"

"Follow me," I tell him, as I head to the back corner of Tommy's backyard. I start climbing the ladder to his tree house.

"Seriously, Nathan, I know you like to go up to the tree house when you need to think through a problem, but now is not the time!" Tommy yells.

I look back down at him and sigh. "Well? Are you guys coming or what?"

"Shoot," Tommy mumbles, before following me up the ladder. Sam follows closely behind. "We really don't have time for this. My parents are going to be home soon and ..."

I shine my flashlight into the tree house as Tommy peeks over my shoulder. There on the floor is Andy, fast asleep. I can hear Tommy let out a sigh of relief. He whispers, "Come on, I'll carry him down."

Tommy steps around me and kneels over Andy. Poor kid probably fell asleep while he was waiting for us to find him. We carefully carry him down the steps and back into the house.

Mr. and Mrs. Jensen come home shortly after we get Andy to bed. There is no mention of our hide and seek game or the fact that we lost Andy. They give Tommy, Sam, and me each four dollars. I say a quick goodbye before swiftly heading out the door.

"So how did it go?" Mom asks, as I enter the kitchen. "You look a little worn out. Did everything go okay?"

"I guess," I answer. Right now all I really want to do is go to sleep.

"Not so easy is it, Nathan?" Abby sneers, as she walks into the room.

"It was fine." I am in no mood for Abby's know-it-all attitude. Not that I ever am in the mood, but if I had to pick between tonight and a different night, tonight is not the night I'd choose.

Abby laughs. "Well, I've babysat for Andy before. He may look all sweet and cute, but trust me—he's not. You want to be his babysitter? I say go for it. Just don't let him talk you into playing hide and seek."

Uh, yeah, it would have been nice if she had given me that little piece of advice *before* I went over to Tommy's house to babysit. "Don't worry, Abby, I'm not taking over as Andy's babysitter," I say definitively. "We were just trying to raise money for our fifth grade New York City trip, but we only made four dollars each. There's no way we can make enough money babysitting. We'll have to try something else."

There. That sounded like a good enough reason to tell Abby and Mom why I didn't want to babysit anymore. After all, I couldn't exactly tell them that three eleven-year-olds couldn't keep track of one six-year-old. I certainly couldn't tell them that I was doodling and daydreaming while Tommy and Sam were playing video games, giving Andy the perfect opportunity to run outside all by himself and climb a tall ladder in the dark. Nope, I'll just have to stick to the story that at four dollars a pop, it would take us months to raise the money for our school trip. It's not like I'm not telling the truth, because I am. It will take us months to raise enough money if all we're going to get is four dollars each time. I'm just omitting some other pieces of information, that's all.

"Is that why you wanted to babysit?" Abby asks, laughing.

"Why's that so funny?" I demand.

"It's not funny, Nathan. It's very admirable," Mom says.

"Yeah, except you wasted your time," Abby adds.

"What do you mean?" I ask. I know it is only four dollars, but it's better then nothing.

"School fundraising has to be fundraising by the school, *duh*!" Abby mocks.

"What are you talking about?" I ask. I swear Abby makes zero sense sometimes. Scratch that. Abby makes zero sense most of the time.

"Nathan," Mom explains, "fundraising for a school trip has to be part of a school event. Individually doing odd jobs here and there, like babysitting, doesn't actually count. I mean, yes, it counts for you, but it's not part of the trip money. For that, everyone has to work together. I'm afraid that even if you did make enough money babysitting, you wouldn't have been able to use it towards the trip. I thought you knew that."

"Apparently not," Abby says. "Nice work, butthead."

"All right, Abby, that's enough. Don't you have homework to finish?"

"Fine. I'm just wasting brain cells trying to explain it to him anyway."

"Abby, I said enough. Now go." Mom points to the stairs, and we watch as Abby slithers off.

I sit down at the kitchen table and put my head down on my arms.

"Nathan, trust me, there's plenty of time for your class to make money. You've got the big Halloween party next week, remember?"

"I'm not in the mood for a party," I say, not looking up. "I really wanted to go to New York City."

"I know! That's what I'm talking about. The Halloween party next week is one of the biggest fundraisers the school does. The school gets money for tickets, food, drinks – everything, and all the money the school makes goes towards your trip. In fact, the school usually makes more than enough money just from the Halloween party alone to go towards it. You'll see; you will have no trouble at all getting to New York City."

"I sure hope so," I say.

"Oh don't worry about it, Nathan. Boy, you sure do look exhausted. What were you doing over there anyway, running laps around the block or something?"

"Yeah, something like that," I tell Mom.

Chapter 7

"Mom! Hey, Mom! Are you home?"

"I'm in the kitchen, Nathan," Mom yells.

"Oh hi, Mom," I say, completely out of breath, having run home from the school bus stop. "Can I go over to Tommy's house...what's that smell?" I try to smile and not gag at the same time. *Please don't let that be my dinner. Please let me go to Tommy's house for dinner tonight...and for the rest of my life.*

"Nathan, you're just in time! I was just testing out some recipes. I'm in charge of the snacks for the school Halloween party this year."

"Oh...great." Didn't Mom say the snacks were a big part of the fundraiser? Maybe someone else should be in charge of the food. I wonder if Tommy's mom has some free time to bake some stuff.

"Right now I'm working on something called Brain Pudding – it's in the oven. Do you want to try some? It should be ready in just a few minutes."

"Uh, no thanks," I say, trying to smile, "that delicious lunch you packed me really filled me up." I pat my stomach – a feeble attempt to make my lie a bit more authentic.

"Well, I know how much you love my tuna

casserole. We still have some left. I can heat it up for you for dinner if you want."

"Oh, well it sounds great, Mom, but I was kind of going to ask if I could go over to Tommy's house. His mom invited me over for dinner." The truth is, Tommy asked if I could come over after school, but given this newfound information about my pending dinner, I'm sure I could manage to stay at Tommy's to eat as well.

"But you're going to miss my Witches' Eyeball Brew."

"Did somebody say Eyeball Brew?" Dad cheerfully bounds into the kitchen.

"Oh, hi, Dad. I didn't know you were home."

"Hi, Nathan. Our offices are getting painted, so I'm working from home today. Something sure does smell good in here."

"That would be my Brain Pudding!" Mom says with a big smile.

"Brain Pudding? Eyeball Brew? Don't tell me—the school Halloween party must be coming up. Hey, Nathan, did I ever tell you about the time Uncle Robert and I dressed up like vampires?"

"You mean the time when you snuck into Grandmom and Grandpop's bedroom in the middle of the night and scared them half to death?" I ask.

"Grandmom screamed so loud, the neighbor called the police. Grandpop was not happy." Dad snaps out of his remember-when memory and looks straight into my eyes. "Now don't you get any ideas about trying something like that, Nathan. I sleep with one eye open, you know. All of us vampires do." Dad winks and leaves the room.

"So can I, Mom?"

"Can you what, Nathan?"

"Can I go over to Tommy's house?"

"Sure, Nathan."

"Thanks, Mom!" I race upstairs to grab my sweatshirt.

"Hey, watch it nerd face!" Abby yells, as I pass her in the hallway.

"I'm not bothering you. What's your problem anyway?"

I should just ignore her, get my sweatshirt, and walk over to Tommy's house as planned. But for some unexplainable reason, I stop to talk to my annoying big sister.

"*My problem* is that thanks to *you*, I have to go to the stupid fifth grade Halloween dance. I'm in eighth grade! I can't be seen at some *baby* dance! Thanks a lot, *Nathan*."

"How's that my fault?" *Stop talking, Nathan! Just get your sweatshirt and walk away.*

"Because, Mom wants me to go with her to help. If you weren't in fifth grade, or here at all for that matter, I wouldn't have to go." And with that, Abby turns on her heels and marches down the hallway. "Well there is one bright side," Abby says, turning around one more time before reaching her bedroom. "At least *I* don't have to go with Lisa Crane." A smug smile appears on her face. "Didn't you know? I overheard Mom talking on the phone, and she said you would be *happy* to go to the dance with Lisa. The next thing you know, Mom and Mrs. Crane will be planning your wedding." Abby smirks one more time before slamming her bedroom door shut.

Wedding?! Lisa Crane?! Just the sound of her name causes my entire body to shudder—and not in a good way. There's no way I'm taking that bratty know-it-all to the Halloween Dance or anywhere... ever. In fact, I'm not taking any girl to the school dance. I don't even like girls! What is wrong with Mom? Just because Lisa's mom is Mom's best friend, doesn't mean she gets to plot out my life. I grab my sweatshirt and run back down the stairs.

"Mom! Mom! MOM!"

"I'm still in the kitchen, Nathan. Why all the screaming? Did you decide you want to try my Brain Pudding after all?" Mom walks toward me with a cup of bubbling mush. I try to hold my breath to keep the putrid smell out and talk at the same time. FYI, it doesn't work.

"Abby just told me I have to take Lisa Crane to the dance. You mean, like a *date?* I'm only eleven! I just want to go and hang out with my friends!"

Mom starts laughing, but honestly, I do not see the humor in this situation. "Oh, Nathan," Mom says, "we're just giving Lisa a ride there and back, that's all. Her parents have a meeting they need to go to that night and won't be around. Don't you worry, there will be plenty of time to date Lisa once you get older."

"What did you say?"

"I said there will be plenty of other kids at the dance Lisa can hang out with once you get there. Are you sure you don't want any Brain Pudding?"

"No thanks, Mom. I'll see you later."

The fresh air only partially helps to get the smell of brains out of my nose. The smell of Tommy's mom's cooking as I walk up their driveway, however, does the trick. I wish there were a way I could politely ask Mom to take some cooking classes from Tommy's mother. Or ask Tommy's mom to invite me over for every meal for the next fifty years. Either option will work fine for me.

"Hi, Nathan," Mrs. Jensen says, as she opens the door. "Tommy told me you were coming over. Would you like to stay for dinner? I'm making homemade pizza."

Hmmm, let me think about that for a minute. "YES! I mean sure. Thanks."

"Oh, good. Tommy's out back. Let him know we'll be eating in an hour."

"Okay. Thanks, Mrs. Jensen." I walk around to the backyard and climb up to the tree house.

"Hey, what are you reading?" I ask.

Tommy looks up. "Mom bought me this book. It's all about werewolves. It's pretty cool actually. Did you know that werewolves have been walking amongst us for thousands of years?"

"Werewolves aren't real. They're just made up— like vampires."

"No, really," Tommy states, "it says so right here: *While many say werewolves originated from European folklore, sightings of actual werewolves date as early as the Ancient Greeks and can be identified by eyebrows which meet at the bridge of the nose and hair growing on the back of the hand.*"

"Ha. That sounds like your Dad!" I say, laughing.

"Very funny, Nathan. Anyway, have you thought about what costume you're going to wear for the school party?"

Halloween costumes are always a bit tricky. Now that Mom has finally agreed I am old enough to figure out my own costume, it's a little easier, not to mention much less embarrassing. But, there is still this rule that I'm not allowed to carry any weapons. I was hoping that my laser tag party might change her mind, but nope, still no weapons. Not even ones made out of cardboard. Whatever. This year, I think I figured out away to get around that.

"I'm going to be a wizard," I proudly announce.

"A what?" Tommy asks.

"A wizard. You know, like a witch, only the boy version. It's pretty cool, actually. Dad gave me an old robe of his, and I cut the bottom off so it's not too long. I have a hat made of some old felt I found in Mom's craft kit, and I made a really cool magic wand out of wire and tin foil."

"But you're not allowed to carry weapons, remember?"

"It's not a weapon, it's a wand. Big difference. At least to my mom." I smile proudly. "What about you? What are you going as?"

"I'm not sure yet," Tommy replies.

"Well, how about a werewolf?"

"No way! Those things really freak me out. There's a story in here about a kid who was wearing a werewolf costume one Halloween when there was a full moon. Well, a real werewolf saw him and

48

attacked him. The bite turned the poor kid into one, too. No thanks."

I shake my head. "Your call."

Chapter 8

Our teacher, Mrs. Cogin, is not happy. Tonight is the Halloween dance, and nobody is paying attention to her. Personally, I don't get why we even have to go to school today. Shouldn't we all be home getting ready? What kind of celebration is it if we have to go to school?

Mrs. Cogin tells us to put our math books away. Instead, she wants us to watch a movie. At least we're supposed to be watching. All I can hear is Lisa Crane going on and on about her costume. It's no wonder Mrs. Cogin is so cranky today.

Lisa says she is going as Cleopatra, the Queen of the Nile. Ever since we started learning about Ancient Egypt in social studies class, Lisa has been obsessed with Cleopatra. If you ask me, I think she should go as a mummy. She could wrap her entire head up in cloth. Not only won't we have to look at her, but she won't be able to speak either. Sometimes my genius just astounds me!

"Okay class," Mrs. Cogin says thirty minutes later, turning off the movie. "It's time for a little class project."

The entire class groans in unison.

"Now, now. This is going to be fun," she continues.

"It's Halloween related. Pick a partner and come up to the front of the room for supplies. The decorating committee for tonight ran a little short on time, so they asked us to help with some posters."

Tommy jabs me in the side. "I'll go grab the stuff we need."

At least we get to pick our partners. Last time I had a project to do with a partner, I was stuck with Lisa. It did not end well. Drawing posters I can handle. Maybe today won't be so bad after all.

As we settle back into our seats, Tommy and I decide to make our posters look like the inside of a haunted mansion. Tommy is drawing the background with spider webs and cracked windows, and I'm drawing scary faces. Honestly, it's really not that spooky looking, but there is only so much you can do with a poster and markers. I finish up a picture of a giant cauldron for my witches' brew before Mrs. Cogin announces that time is up.

I volunteer to carry all the posters down to the gym while everyone else helps to clean up. Mr. Sparks, the janitor, runs up to me in a panic.

"Nate! Thank goodness. I've been looking everywhere for you! They need your help in the gym right away."

"I know, I'm heading there now," I reply. Seriously, if everyone hadn't waited until the last minute, none of this decorating stuff would be a problem.

"Be careful, son," Mr. Sparks says, as he pushes me through the door.

I enter the dark gym. "Hello?" I call out. The doors slam shut with a bang behind me, eliminating what little light there was. I thought there were windows in here. Why is it so dark? I feel along the walls for the light switch, but can't find it. "Anyone?" I lean the posters against the wall. Where is everyone? Shouldn't there be people in here setting up for the dance? I thought Mom said she was coming this afternoon to help. What's that awful smell?

"Ah, I've been expecting you," says the somewhat odd yet familiar shrill voice.

"Lisa? Is that you? What's wrong with your voice, and why is it so dark in here?"

A tiny spark glimmers from across the room. The flame jumps, lighting a row of candles along the back wall. Candles? I guess people *were* busy decorating today. Nice touch. A girl dressed all in black seems to be floating toward me through the darkness.

"So, it is Nate Rocks after all," she says, as she approaches.

My eyes focus on her face. "What are you doing in the gym, Lisa, and why are you dressed like an ugly witch? I thought you wanted to be Cleopatra."

"Ugly witch!?" she shrieks. She lifts the wand she is holding and swirls it in the air. A ring of fire appears at my feet, surrounding me.

"Uh, perhaps ugly was a bit strong?" I meekly respond. "I just meant, you look different than usual, that's all. Could you call off the flames? I'm just here to help set up."

She lifts her wand and flicks her wrist. The flames instantly disappear.

"That's pretty cool. I didn't know they were going

to have special effects tonight. Can you show me how you did that, Lisa?"

"My name is Lizetta, not Lisa, and I do not need your help. But perhaps they do ..." Lisa once again raises her wand. A light jumps from its tip to the other corner of the gym, lighting that part of the room.

"Mom? Dad? Abby? What are you all doing here? Lisa, why are they tied up? Is this some kind of a joke?"

"I told you, my name is Lizetta!" Lizetta flicks her wand once more, lighting the rest of the candles along the other three walls. What used to be the gym now appears to be a very old and spooky looking castle.

"All righty then," I say, slowly backing up, "Lizetta it is."

"Help us!" Abby screams.

"Silence!" Lizetta orders. She lifts her wand again and mumbles some words I don't quite understand. A large puff of smoke appears. Mom and Dad are now standing next to Lizetta, Mom is dressed as another witch, and Dad is dressed as a vampire. They both have glazed eyes and evil grins on their faces. Abby, still in the corner, is tied up.

"What did you do to them?" I demand.

Lizetta just laughs.

"Nate!" Abby yells from across the room. "Don't just stand there! Do something!"

Lizetta turns to her.

"You! I thought I told you to be quiet!" Lizetta commands. She points her wand at Abby and says,

53

"Goblins and ghouls I know the most, turn that whiny teen into a ghost!"

"Now we're talking," I mumble under my breath.

Lizetta taps her wand in the air. Another puff of smoke clouds my view. When it finally clears, all that is left where Abby was standing is a monkey.

"Abby? Uh, Lizetta, I think you might have gotten that spell wrong."

"Oh, I can fix that," Mom says, walking over to the steaming cauldron. She begins chanting over the green bubbling liquid. She then fills a cup with the glowing substance and brings it over to Abby. "Drink," she instructs, tipping the cup into Abby's furry mouth.

"Abby! No! Don't drink it! That's Mom's Witches' Eyeball Brew! Trust me...Do. Not. Drink. It!"

The monkey, I mean Abby, takes a big gulp of the concoction. Sparks fly from her fur as she instantly transforms into a lizard.

"Hmm," Mom says, handing the cup to Lizetta, "that didn't seem to work so well either."

"Perhaps she needs a vampire's bite," Dad says in a strange, trying to be creepy but not quite working, voice.

"Hey, what's going on in here?" Tommy asks, entering the room.

"Tommy, no! Run! Go get help!" I yell. The door slams shut behind him. A cross bolt falls in front of the door, locking us all inside.

"Happy Halloween?" Tommy says quietly, backing into a corner.

"Ahh," Lizetta says, walking over to Tommy. "Just

what I need."

"N-n-n-eed?" Tommy stammers.

"Yes," Lizetta says, tapping her wand in the palm of her hand. "You will make a perfect werewolf."

"W-w-w-erewolf?"

"What's the matter boy? Why do you keep repeating me? Yes, that's right, werewolf. Then all I need is a mummy," Lizetta states, turning to look at me, "and my creature army will be complete. We'll take over the school first, then the town, the state, the country, and the world! Mwahahahaha...Although, I'm still not quite sure what to do about the lizard. No matter. Now, where was I? Oh yes. Mwahahahaha."

Lizetta lifts her wand, about to put a spell on Tommy. There has to be a way I can get Lizetta's wand away from her. Think, Nate! Think!

Of course! The posters – that's it! I reach my hand behind me and grab one of the posters without being noticed. I have no time to waste. If I don't get this right the first time, we are all doomed. I take a deep breath, quietly lift the poster, and swiftly whirl it out of my hand like a Frisbee. It flies through the air, spinning at top speed, although it seems to me as if it is going in slow motion.

"Lizetta! Watch out," Mom warns.

Lizetta turns and puts both hands up to protect her face. The poster slams into her hands, causing her to release the wand, which drops to the floor and rolls across the room. Dad and I both dive towards it, but I am seconds ahead of him. I grab the wand and point it at the group. Abby slithers next to me. Tommy runs over to me as well.

"Big deal," Lizetta says, smirking, "it's not like you know how to use that thing."

I point the wand to Mom and Dad and chant, *"Wizards and wands aren't all that bad, turn these creatures back to Mom and Dad."*

With a puff and a crackle, Mom and Dad lose their costumes and are wearing the clothes they had on this morning. They run over to me and give me a hug.

"Thank you, Nate! Thank you!"

"Ah, beginner's luck," Lizetta responds.

I point the wand to Lizetta. "Oh yeah? Well try this one on for size: *Tricks and trouble are not all that funny, it's time to turn Lisa into a mummy!"*

Out of the ceiling, strips of fabric appear, wrapping Lizetta up tightly.

"Mmmm! Mmmm!" she yells, unable to speak as the material covers her mouth.

"Awesome," Tommy says.

Mom taps me on the shoulder. "Nate? What about Abby?"

I look over to my lizard sister as she slides her tongue in an out.

"Nate?" Mom repeats.

"Uh, Nathan, why are you drawing Abby as a lizard? I don't think that's what Mrs. Cogin really had in mind when she asked us to make the decorations for the dance tonight," Tommy says, staring at the poster I'm working on.

I don't know, I think to myself, I think it kind of suits her.

Chapter 9

"What's the big hold up?" I lean over to ask Tommy.

Moments before, the telephone in Mrs. Cogin's classroom rang. After a brief conversation, Mrs. Cogin announced that she had to go down to the office for a few minutes. The whole thing was a little odd if you ask me. We're supposed to be working on our math assignment, but of course everyone is now talking instead. Mrs. Cogin rarely leaves us alone for this very reason. Last time she had to go to the office, she came back so mad that I swear there was steam coming out of her ears. She said she could hear us chatting all the way down the hall. She told us that if we did it again, we'd all have to stay in and clean the classroom instead of going outside for recess. Believe me, no one wants that to happen, especially me now that I actually like going out for recess.

Still, no one seems to care, although this time, we've all got the talking down to a whisper. Well, everyone except Lisa. Miss Goody Two Shoes is of course busy working on the math assignment. Either that or she's writing down all the names of everyone who is *not* working on math so she can give it to Mrs. Cogin as soon as she returns. Come to think of it, I'd be willing to bet that is exactly what Lisa is doing, because in between writing, she keeps turning around to glare at me. Have I mentioned lately that Lisa annoys me to no end?

Tommy shrugs and looks back down at his math book. Guess he doesn't want to get on Lisa's list, but I don't care. I want to know what's going on. It's been two whole weeks since the Halloween dance, and there's been no word on how much money we raised or if it's even enough to cover our New York trip. Am I the only one who realizes how important this information is? Surely I can't be the only one who wants to go on this trip! I mean, the Halloween dance was fun and all, but it had a purpose much greater than just dressing up and hanging out.

Actually, the Halloween dance was more fun than I was expecting. I'm not sure, but I think we had a pretty good turn out. See, it was kind of hard to tell because Mom insisted we get there early so we could help with the food set up. If you ask me, I think she just wanted to get there early to make sure her Brain Pudding and Eyeball Brew had a spot front and center on the snack table.

There weren't many kids there yet when we arrived, so I helped hang some random decorations in the gym, while Abby sat on the bleachers making faces at us in between text messages. Once Tommy and Sam showed up, we went outside to hang out by the swings. We weren't supposed to, but honestly I had no choice. Lisa was clinging to me like a rat on cheese. I think she actually thought I was her date!

Thankfully, after a few minutes, she announced she was hungry. She looked at me like *I* was suppose to go get her some food or something, but instead, I gave her the same look back and told her all the food was set up against the back wall. She went off in a huff. That's when Tommy, Sam, and I made our great escape outside. Luckily, Lisa didn't come looking for us.

I knew Mom wouldn't even notice. She always volunteers to "chaperone" these things, but then when she actually gets to the event, she barely pays attention. She's always too busy talking to all the other chaperones. Abby was supposed to be helping chaperone as well, but it was no surprise that she also disappeared. In fact, she left the gym even before Tommy, Sam, and I did. I'm still not sure where she went off to, but it was probably to find better cell phone reception.

Anyway, it was pretty warm outside for October, so Tommy, Sam, and I stayed on the playground for most of the party. By the time we made it back inside, most of the other kids were gone already. That's why I'm really not sure if there was a packed house or not, but according to Mom there were a ton of kids.

Unfortunately, I know for a fact that Mom's food didn't sell well. I can't really blame anyone there. I suppose it didn't take long for word to spread to everyone to stay away from the Brain Pudding and Eyeball Brew. I'm just hoping that the other food sales were enough to make up for it. This dance is our ticket to New York City. So yeah, I'm kind of worried about how the party went.

On the upside, my costume was totally awesome. Mom didn't even question the whole wand thing. Between laser guns and now the wand, I feel like I'm making some good progress. I'm thinking next year I may be able to go all out and wear a tinfoil sword, or maybe she'll finally let me get that super soaking water gun I've been wanting for the past five years.

"But do you think we made enough money?" I ask just a bit louder, trying to get Tommy to pay attention to me.

"Enough money for what, Nathan?" Mrs. Cogin asks, as she walks in the door.

Great. Looks like Lisa can save her list – even without it I probably just bought myself a recess inside re-arranging Mrs. Cogin's supply cabinet.

"Uh...um...well ..." I stammer.

"You are wondering about the school trip to New York, aren't you?" she asks, not looking nearly as mad as I was expecting.

"Yes, ma'am," I say in my best *I didn't mean to directly disobey you, and I really want to go out for recess* voice.

"Well," she says, sitting behind her desk. "I was going to wait until after lunch to discuss this, but now is as good a time as any. I'm afraid the Halloween dance didn't do quite as well as we were hoping."

I drop my head to my desk as the class groans.

"I was just meeting with the principal down in the office. I'm sorry to say that according to Mrs.

Simmons, we will need to raise one thousand dollars by the time we break for the December holidays or the trip is off."

"A thousand dollars!" I jump to my feet yelling. I can feel my cheeks getting all red as I slide back down into my seat. That's it. I guess we can all just kiss the trip to New York goodbye. Looks like fifth-grade is going to be a total wash.

"I'm afraid so, Nathan," Mrs. Cogin says. "It's a very expensive trip, and the school can only afford to chip in a third of the cost this year. Unfortunately, we've had a lot of budget cuts. The Halloween dance helped with some of the extra, but not all. Trust me, you are not the only one upset about this. I look forward to the New York City trip every year myself."

"Well, what if we split up the difference and have the kids going on the trip each pay their share? Didn't we have to pay ten dollars each last year to go to the apple orchid?" Lisa asks.

"Lisa," Mrs. Cogin says, "every student already paid twenty-five dollars last month to reserve their spot. It is school policy not to ask for more than that. It wouldn't be fair to the families who couldn't afford it. We want everybody to be able to go on this trip."

This time Lisa jumps up. "But that's not fair! Are you saying that *I* won't be able to go on the trip even if *I* can pay my *own* way?"

"Yes, Lisa, that's correct. But..."

Ooh, here it comes! This is the part where Mrs. Cogin gets so aggravated with Lisa that she winds up embarrassing her in front of the whole class. I bite my lip to keep from smiling as I wait for it. I'm telling you, I live for days like this!

"... since you are so concerned about it, why don't you lead up a committee to work on how the class will raise the money for the trip."

Hahahaha.

Mrs. Cogin continues, "I'd like you to put together a team of two or three people. You can all brainstorm on some fundraising ideas for us to do as a class. I have complete faith in you, Lisa. I know you'll be able to come up with some great events to help us raise enough money so we can *all* go to New York City this spring."

"Yes, Mrs. Cogin," Lisa replies smugly, sitting tall in her seat. "I'm the perfect person to handle this. Thank you for picking me. Your trust means so much, and I won't let you down."

Wait a minute! That's not embarrassing at all! That is the complete opposite of embarrassing. Did Mrs. Cogin just make Lisa in charge of the fundraising committee? Is she crazy? Why in the world would she do that? Now we'll have to do something dumb like sell flowers or butterflies or something, and Lisa will be walking around with an even bigger attitude than usual! This is horrible.

"NO!" I burst out, as I jump back out of my seat.

"Nathan? Is there a problem?"

I nudge Tommy to get up also. Now is the time for us to stick together and stand up to Lisa, once and for all. We've got to let Mrs. Cogin know that having Lisa involved in raising the money for our school trip is just about the worst idea anyone can come up with. In fact, it's a guarantee that *none of us* will get to go on this trip. Seriously! Thankfully, Tommy stands up. I knew there was a good reason he was my best friend. Mrs. Cogin likes Tommy. She'll listen to him. There's no way, Lisa can be in charge of the fundraising committee or even on the fundraising committee. I know Tommy will tell her. There is just no way ...

"Mrs. Cogin," Tommy begins.

That's right, Tommy, you tell her. Tell her that Lisa is absolutely the worst choice for the fundraising committee. Tell her that no one will want to work with Lisa. Tell her.

"Nathan and I would like to work on the committee with Lisa."

What did he just say? He was supposed to put Lisa in her place, not offer to work with her. I stare at Tommy and blink my eyes. I must be dreaming. That's really the only logical answer here. This seriously cannot be happening.

"Thank you, boys," Mrs. Cogin says. "I think that is an excellent idea."

Tommy nudges me back as if I'm supposed to be proud of him or something – and it hurt, too. I am definitely *not* dreaming. Great. Yeah, *excellent idea*, I think to myself, as I see Lisa's squinty eyes staring at me.

Chapter 10

"What were you thinking?" I ask Tommy, as we make our way over to our lunch table.

"What?" Tommy replies. "Isn't that why you nudged me to stand up with you—to help keep Lisa from being in charge of the committee?"

"Well, yes, but I was hoping you'd say something to convince Mrs. Cogin that Lisa shouldn't be on the committee. I wasn't expecting you to volunteer us to be on the committee with her! Now we have to work with Lisa. Do you know what this means?"

"Um, that we have to work with Lisa?"

I roll my eyes. "Yes," I say, "but didn't you hear what Mrs. Cogin said? The three of us have to meet every Tuesday and Thursday afternoon during recess for the next month and a half. This is just awful!"

"Sorry, I figured if we were on the committee with Lisa, then we'd be able to keep an eye on her. You know, make sure she doesn't have us doing something dumb to raise money, like sell unicorns or rainbows or something," Tommy says, pulling out his lunch.

It's funny how Tommy and me are able to think so alike at times and yet so differently at other times.

But, I guess he sort of makes sense...kind of. I'm still upset, though.

I check out Tommy's lunch, and my mouth begins to water. His mom made him a turkey and cheese sandwich on one of those potato rolls I love, with some of her homemade coleslaw. I look down at my own gourmet meal. A Tupperware container full of ... Um, actually, I have no idea what this is. It resembles some sort of meat, and it's sitting in what I think is supposed to be tomato sauce. Except it doesn't look or smell like tomato sauce. It looks and smells more like the sludge from the bottom of the lake at camp. I quickly put the lid back on the container and pull out the package of cheese and crackers I grabbed when Mom wasn't looking this morning.

"We need a plan," I state. "We need to think up a way to keep Lisa out of our hair while we figure out how to raise enough money to go on this trip. One false move by Lisa and she could ruin the entire thing."

"I've got it! We can lock Lisa in the supply cabinet for the next two months," Tommy says, with an oddly serious look on his face.

"Hmm. As much as I'd like to do that, I'm pretty sure someone might notice. It may take a few days, but still. Perhaps we need something a little less drastic. We need to come up with a great fundraising idea; otherwise, Lisa will have us set up in some sort of kissing booth." I shudder just thinking about it.

"A kissing booth? Oh that's a good one! Maybe we could put Lisa in it and watch her turn into a frog after someone kisses *her*." Tommy is laughing so hard he clutches his stomach.

I try to picture it in my head. That would be pretty awesome. Doubtful, but awesome.

"Listen, Nathan," Tommy says after calming down, "don't worry so much! We're a committee of three, remember? We can out vote her two to one on any idea we don't like. And we can pass any idea we do like even if she hates it. It'll be like she doesn't even exist since we'll always have our two votes to her one vote. I think it was a brilliant idea on my part if you ask me."

"Maybe, but knowing Lisa, she'll find a way around that, like asking for a class vote or something. I wouldn't get too confident. We definitely need to come up with something spectacular that is a guaranteed money maker."

"Talking fundraising without me?" the piercing voice asks from behind my back.

Lisa sits down at our table without waiting for an invitation.

"That's Sam's seat," I say, wishing more than ever that Sam would hurry through the hot lunch line.

"Really?" Lisa replies, "I don't see him anywhere."

"He's getting his lunch," Tommy explains. "He'll be here any minute."

"Don't worry," Lisa says, "I'm not staying. I just wanted to give you this." She puts a piece of paper down on the table.

"What's this for?" I ask, picking it up.

Lisa rolls her eyes and sighs. "Fundraising guidelines. See? At the top of the page? It says,

67

Fundraising Guidelines." She reads the title extra slowly to make her point.

I shoot Tommy a glare as he begins to chuckle. He abruptly stops and looks down at his sandwich.

"I know that, Lisa. I can read," I say. Really? First you have to take up all my recess time, and now you have to annoy me at lunch, too? "I meant, why are you giving this to us. We don't meet until later."

"Well, Mrs. Cogin wanted you to have it to look over before our first meeting. She thought maybe you two could jot down some ideas before we meet. Do you think you can handle that?" she asks, sticking a pencil in front of my face.

"Yeah. I got it," I say, grabbing the pencil. Thankfully, Lisa stands up and walks away.

"Ribbit," Tommy says, as Lisa leaves. Well, he tries to ribbit, but since he has a mouthful of food, it just comes out sounding like a big burp instead. Still completely hysterical though.

Lisa turns to look at us and says, "Boys...ugh," before quickly storming off.

"See what I mean?" I say to Tommy. "Having to spend all that extra time with Lisa is going to be pure torture!" I look back down at the paper.

"So what does it say?" Tommy asks.

"It just says that we have to work together to find an activity that everyone can participate in and that our teacher has final say to our ideas. It also says that we are meeting three days a week now!" I shut my eyes tightly and open them back up just to make sure. Yup, it definitely says three days a week.

"What? This is getting out of control!" Tommy says.

"Yeah, two days is bad enough! There's no way I'm missing three days of recess every week to hang out with Lisa Crane! We need our fresh air! We're just kids—we're still growing!" I take my pencil and cross out the word *three* and write in *two*.

Suddenly, the fire alarm goes off. Not again! Why do we always have to have fire drills during lunch? Why can't we ever have them during math or science? I get up from the table to follow the crowd of kids outside. We're supposed to walk single file, but that never happens. As I walk toward the door with the crowd of other kids, I can feel someone tugging at my arm.

"Mrs. Simmons?"

The principal puts her finger up to her mouth to let me know I should be quiet.

"But, I was being quiet, and it wasn't my fault I wasn't in line. There is no line. Why am I in trouble?"

She pulls me into the hallway. "You're not in trouble," she says. "We need your help!"

"Why? Is there really a fire? Oh wow! This isn't a drill at all, is it?" I look around, trying to see signs of smoke or flames.

"No, Nate, there is no fire," she says, "but you are correct. This isn't a drill. We have a true emergency. I pulled the alarm to get everyone out of the building, and now I need your help!"

"What's going on?" I ask.

"We have a bit of a situation. It seems we had a

little mishap in the science lab."

Science lab? We were just in there this morning with our science teacher, Mrs. Ivy, observing the tadpoles we caught in the pond behind the school last week. So far, no sign of any frogs.

"What happened?" I ask.

"It's kind of a long story, and we don't have a lot of time," Mrs. Simmons says. "But somehow the frogs escaped."

"Wow, that was fast! They were just tadpoles this morning."

"Yeah, freaky," Mrs. Simmons says, "but that's not the point. The point is, once the frogs got out, they knocked over a bottle of Mrs. Ivy's perfume."

I cringe. Nothing smells worse than Mrs. Ivy's perfume. Nothing. I don't think Mrs. Cogin likes it either, because whenever we walk into the science room, the first thing she does is crack open the window. Then she turns on the big fan Mrs. Ivy keeps in the corner to help air out the room. As soon as Mrs. Ivy comes back in, she shuts the fan off. Mrs. Cogin always acts like she doesn't know who turned on the fan and blames it on the class before us. Sometimes that Mrs. Cogin is okay.

"Turns out the perfume is deadly," Mrs. Simmons says.

"You're telling me," I mumble.

"Nate, we need your help! The science lab is behind the cafeteria. The vents to the two rooms directly connect. The fumes from the perfume are heading straight for the cafeteria, and if they make it in there, well...I don't want to think about it."

"I'm confused. What's the big deal if the fumes get into the cafeteria? Everyone is safe outside, breathing fresh air. Can't we just open the doors and windows to air the place out?"

"Don't you get it, Nate?" she asks, clearly losing patience with me. "It's not that simple! The cafeteria is where the kitchen is. It's lunchtime, Nate. The ovens, burners, griddles, and fryers— they're all on. All it takes is for those deadly fumes to hit a flame from the stove and—POOF." Mrs. Simmons claps her hands together for effect. "Even if we shut everything down, there will still be a chance of a spark or some residue gas from these old appliances. I don't mean to alarm you, but even without chemicals, these old stoves could blow at any moment. Please, Nate! You've got to do something and quickly!"

"Me? Why me?" I ask.

"Well because you're Nate Rocks, of course! Now hurry!"

As I tap my fingers on my head to think, I notice that I am now wearing one of those white HAZMAT suits I've seen guys on television wear whenever they need to be protected from pollutants in the air. At least I won't have to breathe in that perfume anymore, but what can I do to stop the fumes from getting in the cafeteria? I look up to the vent. There has to be a way to seal it off. Think, Nate, think!

That's it!

"Quick!" I instruct. "Go into the science lab and open the windows. Then, turn on the big fan in the corner and hold it up to the vent. Make sure it is pointing toward the open windows. I'm going to block off the fumes from getting into the cafeteria so they'll have nowhere to go except back through the science lab. The fan will blow the fumes out the open windows and away from the building. Once outside, they'll safely disintegrate. Trust me."

Mrs. Simmons, also now in a HAZMAT suit, runs out the door and toward the science lab.

Now, to plug up that hole. I run back over to my lunch table and find the container of food Mom packed me for lunch. Yup, this will work perfectly. I climb up on the counter so I can reach the vent. Using a spatula I found on a nearby shelf, I spread Mom's sludge over the openings in the vent. The dark brown substance bubbles for a second before hardening up just like cement. No wonder I always feel like I have a brick in my stomach after eating Mom's cooking! Within minutes, the vent is sealed. "Nothing can get through that stuff," I mumble, jumping off the counter. The stove next to me begins to rumble, blows a small puff of smoke, and then settles down. The school should really think about replacing those.

As I run back into the lab, I see green fumes being pushed out the windows with the help of the fan. By the time the vapors are above the trees they are completely dissolved.

"You did it, Nate! You did it!" Mrs. Simmons exclaims, giving me a hug. "You saved us all from being poisoned! You're a true hero, Nate Rocks!"

"Nathan! Will you stop drawing pictures and

listen to me?"

"Huh?" I look up just as Tommy eats the last of his sandwich.

"I had an idea, you know, to make money. We could have a bake sale! I'll bet we could even use the kitchen here to make stuff."

"Good idea," I say, "only I think we'd better do the cooking at home instead. I heard the ovens here don't work so well."

Chapter 11

"Did you have a chance to read through the handout?" Mrs. Cogin asks.

I nod, looking out the window, watching the rest of my class as they have fun playing outside at recess. This is so unfair. Tommy and I are stuck inside with Lisa and Mrs. Cogin for our first meeting as the official fundraising committee.

"Well," Mrs. Cogin continues, "let's start by throwing out some ideas."

"A fashion show!" Lisa blurts.

"What?" I question.

"It's perfect," she says, gloating. "We can get some of the area stores to donate clothes. Then we can charge admission, walk down the runway, and sell the clothes at the event. All we need is one big designer label, and we've got our thousand dollars right there."

"A thousand dollars for clothes? Nobody is going to pay that!" I say. Really, where does she come up with this stuff?

"You obviously know nothing about high fashion," she says, as she rubs the fabric of my shirt between her fingers. Gross. Now I'll have to throw this shirt out.

74

I pull away from her...next meeting Tommy can sit next to her. Lisa glares at me. Honestly, she is starting to act more and more like Abby everyday. What is it with girls?

"But only the girls are going to be interested in that. What about us boys?" Tommy asks.

"We can have boys clothes, too," Lisa explains. "I *suppose* you and Nathan can model them on the runway, although you two weren't exactly my first choice. No offense, but we're trying to raise money here."

"Forget it," I announce. "I'm not modeling any clothes, and I'm not going to some dumb fashion show."

"All right, all right," Mrs. Cogin says. "Lisa, I think it's a good idea, but the boys do have a point. We need to come up with something that everyone will enjoy. It's a class event, remember? I'm not so sure the boys are going to be very interested in fashion. At least not yet."

What does she mean *yet*? I'm never going to be interested in fashion—that I can guarantee you.

"How about a bake sale?" Tommy asks, proudly.

"I thought about that too, Tommy," Mrs. Cogin states.

Tommy sits up tall, smiling.

"However, there are so many kids in the school with food allergies, I'd hate to have to be responsible for all that. Plus, we'd only be able to sell each item for a quarter tops. That's an awful lot of brownies we'll need to sell to reach a thousand dollars."

"Maybe we need more than one event," I say.

"We could have something in November and then something else in December."

"Nathan," Lisa whines, "we can't even think of *one* event to do for this fundraising thing—although personally I thought I had a great idea—now you want to do *two* events? Seriously?"

"Actually," Mrs. Cogin interjects, "having two events is not a bad idea. Then we don't have to worry about raising a lot of money all at once. But we don't have much time if we're going to plan two things, so we really need to get moving. Any other ideas?"

"A dance-a-thon!" Lisa yells.

Tommy and I both groan at the same time.

"We could get people to pledge different amounts of money depending on how long each person dances. Boys and girls like to dance, and anyone who doesn't want to dance could help do other stuff, like be in charge of decorating, music, or collecting the pledges," Lisa says, getting more and more excited as she explains.

"Well, I do like that idea ..." Mrs. Cogin starts.

Oh no.

"... but we just had our Halloween dance. I'm afraid our students might be all danced out."

Phew. The last thing we need is another dance. I know my mom would somehow figure out a way to make me hang out with Lisa again. It was bad enough the first time when Mom *claimed* Lisa needed a ride. Since Abby insisted on sitting in the front seat, Lisa and I were stuck together in the back of the car, and Dad's car isn't exactly the cleanest back there. He's been saying for a while now that he needs to take it in for a ....

"A car wash!" I stand up and yell.

"Nathan," Lisa begins, "it's November. It's too cold for a car wash."

"Exactly!" I say, smiling.

"What?" she asks. "You're not making any sense at all."

I turn away from Lisa. "Mrs. Cogin, my dad keeps saying he needs to get his car washed before the snow comes. Something about all the sand and stuff from the roads that will soon be all over his car. I personally don't get it, since his car is just going to get messy again, but he keeps saying now is the time when everyone should get their car washed and ready for winter."

"Come to think of it," Tommy says, "my mom's been saying the same thing."

"You know," Mrs. Cogin says, "it's actually not a bad idea, and it's still pretty warm out. If we work hard to get the word out, I'll bet we can even have it this weekend here in the school parking lot. Yes, I like that idea a lot. Good thinking, Nathan."

"Thanks," I say, smiling. Lisa refuses to look at me, which to be honest is just fine with me anyway.

"Well, we still need something else, and I think I've got a great idea," Lisa says, once again making sure all the attention is back on her.

"What were you thinking of doing, Lisa?" Mrs. Cogin asks.

Let me guess, she wants us to set up a table in the cafeteria to paint people's toenails with glittery nail polish and butterfly decals. Well, that's just not happening because a guy's got to draw the line somewhere you know.

"I was thinking we could make and sell Christmas ornaments," she says. "You know, like the ones they have at the mall every year that are personalized? We could make them in art class out of clay or something. Then we could paint different stuff on them that represent popular hobbies. Things like baseballs and ballet shoes. We'd have a few samples to show, and then we could take orders. We'd personalize them with whatever the buyer wants, and we could also paint the person's name on them as well. They'd make really great gifts," Lisa says, taking a deep breath from talking so fast. "Even boys would like them," she adds, looking at Tommy and me.

"That might actually be a good idea," Tommy says. I kick him under the table. "What?" he asks, looking at me. "My mom loves that sort of stuff for the tree. She'd probably buy one for each member of our family. We could probably get at least $10 for each one—maybe even more. The mall ones are kind of expensive. I remember my mom complaining about that last year."

Lisa is smiling the widest, goofiest smile I've ever seen. I have to admit, it is kind of a good idea. Mrs. Cogin, however, is only half-smiling. It's the same smile she gets when she's about to tell you that you didn't do so well on an assignment. I suddenly have a bad feeling about these ornaments.

"Lisa," Mrs. Cogin says, "I think it's a wonderful

idea, really I do, and it probably would help raise the remainder of the money we need. But I think it would take up too much of our class time, and we're on a pretty tight curriculum schedule—even in art class. Plus, not everyone celebrates Christmas."

Lisa stands up with her hands on her hips. "Well why did you even ask me to be on this committee if you're not going to listen to any of my ideas?" She suddenly starts crying. I've never seen her cry before. I actually kind of feel sorry for her, especially since I liked the whole ornament idea.

"Mrs. Cogin," I begin, "what if we have some sort of school sale where the ornaments are only one of the things we sell. That way, we could just make a few, like after school or something, but have other stuff to sell, too."

"I'm not sure I understand what you're saying, Nathan."

"I'm saying we could have a sale, maybe on the Saturday before our winter break. Lisa and anyone else who is interested can make a bunch of ornaments after school to sell, and everyone else can bring in other stuff that people might want to buy. Tommy, remember that yard sale your parents had last summer while we were at camp?"

"That was awful!" Tommy exclaims. "My parents tried to sell my x-ray glasses! My mom said she didn't realize and that she just thought they were some junky thing I got at a carnival. I mean seriously, how could they send me off to camp and then do something like that? Luckily, nobody bought them. Hey, Nathan, do you still have them? I lent them to you last month, remember?"

"Oh yeah, I thought I might want them for my Halloween costume, but never used them. I'll bring them back to you after school today."

"Can we get back to my ornaments, please?" Lisa demands, suddenly no longer tearful.

"Well, Tommy said his parents made a ton of money from selling all their old stuff, right?" I ask Tommy.

He nods.

"So why can't we do the same thing? It could be like a giant yard sale, only it would be in the school gym instead of the yard."

"A giant gym sale?" Tommy asks.

"Sure," I say, flipping over the paper Mrs. Cogin had given us with the meeting guidelines on it. "We could set it up like this."

I begin mapping out sections of the gym with areas for selling different types of items.

"And I could sell my ornaments?" Lisa asks.

"Hmm," Mrs. Cogin says, "I think that might work. Actually, if we do it more as an auction style, we'll probably bring in even more money. I'm sure we could get people to donate some really great stuff to sell off. And yes, Lisa, you could sell some ornaments."

"Well, I still like my idea the best, but I guess this is better than nothing," Lisa says reluctantly.

I write the word in big letters on top of my paper: AUCTION. "I like it!" I exclaim.

Chapter 12

"Excellent!" Mrs. Cogin exclaims. "Then we're all set. Now we just need to handle the planning. Nathan, would you mind going to the office to make sure we can have the car wash here next weekend? Also, while you're there can you find out if we can hold the auction the weekend before winter break?"

"Sure," I say. "Let me just write that down."

The hallway always seems so quiet when everyone is at recess. I can't believe I have to miss recess twice a week for these meetings. Well, technically three times, but Mrs. Cogin didn't seem to notice that I changed it back to twice a week on the paper, so twice a week it is. I chuckle to myself as I think about Lisa's suggestions. *Fashion Show*. Can you imagine? I push open the door to the office. The desks are gone. In their place are rows and rows of folding chairs all set up. Along the walls, where student artwork and announcements are normally displayed, fancy gold frames with colorful paintings are hanging instead. People are mulling about, looking at the paintings, and talking in low tones. What's up with the paintings and the chairs? Why is everyone so dressed up? Oh no—don't tell me I'm in the middle of a fashion show! I look down to see that I am dressed up as well in a suit and a tie. Yuk, although I must admit, I do look pretty good if I do say so myself. Ha...and Lisa thought I couldn't handle myself on the runway. Of course I can! I start taking long careful strides alongside the paintings, looking left and right with my best serious yet handsome smile, imagining myself walking down a long narrow platform. Personally, I think I'd make a great model.

"Are you okay?" a man I do not recognize asks me. He is wearing a dark suit and dark sunglasses and kind of looks like one of those secret service type men that follow the president around.

"Uh, yeah," I respond, stopping. "Why?"

The man removes an earpiece from his ear. "Well, you kind of have this goofy grin on your face, and you're walking strangely—like you've got rocks in your shoes or something."

I straighten up and bring myself back to reality. "Yeah, I'm fine," I respond.

"Good," the man says, "because we really need your help. The auction is going to start any minute, and we've got to make sure no one leaves with that painting." The man points to the picture hanging in front of us. It's a scene from a baseball game.

"Why can't anyone buy it?" I ask. "I like it. I usually could care less about art, but this would really look great in my room next to my Phillies posters."

"Nate, are you hearing me?" the man asks, sounding annoyed. "Nobody can have it!"

"But why?" I ask, confused. Isn't the whole point of having an auction so that people will buy stuff? It seems kind of rude to ask all these people to come and then tell them they can't buy anything. Sheesh! Even I know that, and I'm only eleven!

The man takes me by the shoulders. "Listen, Nate, we don't have much time. I really need you to pay attention. Nobody can buy that painting, because it's stolen."

"Stolen?!" I yell. "Who are you anyway?"

"Shhh!" The man takes my arm and pulls me into the corner with him. He lowers his voice, "Here's the deal. I'm with INTERPOL—International Police." He quickly flashes a badge at me before hiding it back in his pocket. "You've heard about the big art robbery over in London?"

"Uh, no," I reply.

"Really? You haven't heard about that famous Van Gogh painting being stolen?"

"Van who? Look, I already told you. I'm not really into all that fancy art and stuff. What are you talking about, and what does that have to do with this baseball picture?"

"Van Gogh is a very famous and well respected artist. One of his most valuable paintings was stolen last month. It is worth millions. We believe someone is using this auction as a way to hide it."

"Millions?" I can feel my eyes bulge out of my head. Maybe fancy art isn't so bad after all. "But how?"

The man continues, "Our sources tell us that whoever stole the picture painted a baseball scene over it using special paint that can be removed later to reveal the stolen artwork. We also know that the thief stored the painting in a warehouse with other artwork to temporarily try to hide it. The warehouse manager—unaware of the valuable nature of the painting—donated the artwork, along with several other pieces, to this auction. We believe that our thief will be here in disguise today to bid on the stolen painting."

I look around at the paintings on the wall. "You have noticed that there are three paintings hanging up all with the identical baseball scene on them, haven't you?"

The man nods.

"Well, how will we know which is the stolen one? Won't there be a bunch of different people bidding? How will we know which person is the thief?"

"The paintings are all slightly different," the man explains, leading me back over to get a closer look. He points to each picture. "See? The baseball players up to bat each have different numbers on their backs. The thief knows which one he is going after."

"But do we know which is the stolen painting?"

The man shakes his head. "We don't."

"Then how are we supposed to catch the thief? We just can't go around arresting random people."

"That's where you come in, Nate."

"Me? Why me?"

"Why because you're Nate Rocks, of course! I know you'll think of something. The auction is about to start. We're counting on you, Nate!"

The man replaces his earpiece and walks over to stand in the front corner of the room, leaving me once again alone.

Great. What do I know about figuring out stolen artwork?

"Ladies and gentlemen," a woman with a microphone at the front of the room says, "will you all take your seats? We are ready to begin the auction."

Everyone sits down as each piece of artwork is carefully removed from the walls.

"First up is this lovely floral painting by our own Rachel Andros." The woman waits as the painter takes a quick bow, then continues, "Can we start the bidding at fifty dollars?"

The room becomes a blur as people hold up little signs, and the woman at the front of the room starts raising the price faster and faster: Seventy-five, eighty, eighty-five, ninety. The price keeps going up and up as each person bids. When there is a lull in the bidding, the woman lifts up her hammer and says, "Going once, going twice...SOLD! Two hundred dollars to the man in the blue suit. Thank you, sir. Now for our next item ..."

Wow, two hundred dollars for a painting? We'll have no problem raising the money we need for our New York City trip! One by one the paintings get sold in seconds. It is hard to keep up, and I'm running out of time. The baseball pictures will be for sale soon, and I've got to figure out a way to find out which one is really the stolen painting. If only I could see through that paint. That's it! I slide my hand into my pocket and pull out the glasses.

The auctioneer holds up the first of the three

baseball paintings. She once again starts at fifty dollars. I put on my glasses and wait as she sells the painting for two hundred and fifty dollars. She holds up the second painting. This one sells for two hundred dollars. She holds up the third painting. A man in the back row with a mustache raises his sign a soon as the bidding begins. Was he bidding on the other two paintings as well? I wish I had been paying better attention. Bidding continues, up to three hundred dollars. The auctioneer calls out, "SOLD!"

The man with the moustache starts to make his way to the front of the room.

"NO!" I yell.

Everyone turns to look at me. "Er, I mean ..." I look at the INTERPOL detective and nod. I see him talk into some sort of mouthpiece, and suddenly two other men, dressed the same way and presumably also with INTERPOL, race over to the mustached man. They put handcuffs on him as everyone gasps.

"Are you sure?" the INTERPOL detective asks, as he makes his way over to me.

"Yes," I say, taking off my x-ray vision glasses. I hand them to the detective. "Take a look."

The detective puts the glasses on and looks at the painting. After handing them back to me, he walks over to the man in handcuffs and rips off his moustache.

"Gustov Seline, so it is you after all. Nate Rocks, you are an international hero. The museum in London will be so happy to have their painting back, and an international art thief will finally be put in jail where he belongs. I almost forgot. There is also a reward. You, Nate Rocks, are going to be getting a nice sum of money."

"Money?"

"Yes, Nathan, money...remember? The whole reason we are having the auction?" Lisa yells. "What's wrong with you? Now stop drawing pictures of baseball fields and try to pay attention. Mrs. Cogin was just explaining how the auction would work. You missed the whole thing. How are you supposed to help us if you don't even know how an auction runs?"

"Actually, Lisa, I think I may know a thing or two about auctions after all."

Chapter 13

"You're dreaming if you think I'm going to help out at the car wash this weekend," Abby says, as I explain my weekend plans to Mom after school. "Whose dumb idea was it to even have a car wash, anyway? Everyone knows it's too cold to have a car wash in November."

"It was my idea," I say. "Mrs. Cogin actually thinks it's a great idea, and nobody's asking you to help."

"Of course she'll help," Mom offers. "We all will."

"But, Mom!" Abby shrieks. "I can't wash cars! I'll ruin my nails."

Bobino runs into the kitchen and tries to grab the muffin Abby is eating right out of her hands. "Nathan, can't you control that dog of yours?" She shoves him away.

"Bobino, sit," I say firmly. Bobino trots right over to me and obediently sits. I pat him on his head. "You just don't know how to talk to him," I say. "He thinks you don't like him."

"I don't like him," she replies, sticking her tongue out.

Bobino barks in return. I always knew Bobino was a good judge of character.

"Besides, Mom," Abby continues, "I was thinking

about going to the mall with Emma on Saturday."

"Well, think about going on Sunday instead. In fact, you can take Nathan with you."

"WHAT?" We both yell at the same time.

"Now calm down, both of you. Nathan, didn't you just get done telling me your class is holding an auction next month?" Mom asks.

"Yes, but ..."

"Nathan, you can't have an auction without things to sell. I'll bet there are lots of stores in the mall that would be happy to donate items. You and Tommy can make a flyer to advertise it. Dad can make a bunch of copies at work, and then you boys can pass them around to the different stores. I'm sure once the store managers find out it's for kids, they'll all be jumping at the chance to chip in with something to auction. They love doing stuff like that. It's good publicity for them. Hey, you should bring Lisa with you, too. I can call Marge to see if she is free."

"What? No! Why would we want to bring Lisa?" I ask, feeling my voice getting higher and squeakier.

Abby snickers, causing Bobino to whimper and hide behind a chair.

Mom, oblivious to the entire scene, just keeps right on talking. "Because, Nathan, she's part of your team. Besides, with her great personality, those store managers will be throwing merchandise at her feet."

I'd rather they aim for her head. Isn't it enough that I have to see her all week at school, work with her on this fundraising stuff in place of recess, *and* spend all day Saturday with her at the car wash?

There is no way I'm going to spend my only day off this week hanging out with Lisa Crane. No way, no how, no way ...

"I'll go give her a call now," Mom says, smiling as she walks toward the phone.

"Just great," I mumble.

"What about me?" Abby complains. "Now *my* weekend is completely ruined. Thanks a lot, Nathan."

"What did I do?" I ask. "Trust me, I don't want to go to the mall with you, and I'm also not the one who asked for you to help out at the car wash. Don't be mad at me. Geez. Besides, it's not like you need to watch us at the mall or anything. Tommy and I are more than capable of walking around the mall without a babysitter."

"Don't you mean, Tommy, *Lisa,* and I? Anyway, there won't be any babysitting by me, because the moment we walk in that mall door, I don't know you, Lisa, or Tommy. Get it? If I were an only child, none of this would have happened," Abby says, as she stomps upstairs.

Bobino whimpers again from behind the chair. "Oh, don't be afraid of her," I tell him, grabbing his leash. "Come on, let's go for a walk."

"The mall with Lisa? Is she kidding?" I murmur, as Bobino pulls me down the street.

"Who are you talking to?"

I turn around to see Tommy holding a stack of papers.

"Oh, hi. Just talking to myself I guess." I look at the papers in Tommy's hand. "What are you doing?"

"My mom thought it would be a good idea to make handouts for the car wash and put them in everyone's mailboxes," he replies.

"That's better than my mom's idea," I say. "Need help?"

"Sure," Tommy answers, handing me some flyers.

I wrap Bobino's leash around my wrist to free up my hands.

"So what's your mom's idea?"

"My mom thinks we should go to the mall on Sunday to see if we can get some of the stores to donate stuff for our auction...and she thinks Lisa should come with us."

"Huh? Why does *she* have to come along?"

"Apparently my mom has decided it's her mission to make my life as miserable as possible. Hey, these flyers are pretty good," I say, looking at one before I shove it in Mr. Miller's mailbox. "My mom thinks I should make some for the auction. Want to help?"

"Sure," Tommy replies, as we make our way back down the street. "Let's do it at your house though, Andy's got a bunch of his annoying little friends over right now. To tell you the truth, I was glad my mom suggested I get out of the house. Those little kids were driving me nuts! *Tommy whatcha doin'? Tommy whatcha watchin'? Tommy can we play with you? Tommy whatcha eatin'? Tommy, where ya goin'?* Ugh! I'm surprised none of them asked me to wipe their butt after going to the toilet! I have to tell you, I'm so glad we decided to put an end to that babysitting stuff. I don't think I could have handled it!"

"Yeah, I guess that's the one advantage of having an older sister. She *never* wants to hang out with me. Although, I'd love to see the expression on her face if I asked her to wipe my butt."

Tommy and I crack up laughing as we finish handing out the remaining flyers and head back over to my house. Mom is in the kitchen cooking... um...well, I think it might be...actually, I have no idea what it is, to be honest. I can only pray it's not our dinner.

"Hi, Tommy," she says. "Would you like to stay for dinner? I'm making tacos."

So that's tacos I smell? Ooh, that's not good. Poor Tommy. Nothing good can come out of eating Mom's tacos for dinner. He has no idea what he's about to get himself into. I wish there was a way I could send him some sort of signal. You know, like a tug on my ear could mean *not bad, but avoid the green beans* or wiggling my nose could be *do not eat this food—run for the hills!* Why do I always think of these great ideas when it's too late?

"Oh, yeah. Um, thanks, Mrs. Rockledge. I'd loved to, but my aunt is coming for dinner tonight. Sorry, but thanks for asking."

Phew, Tommy got lucky. The last thing anyone needs to do is eat Mom's tacos for dinner. Trust me. I did it once, and I will never do it again. Thank goodness Mom's television shows are on tonight. Once she starts watching, nothing distracts her. I should be able to sneak into the kitchen later to grab a sandwich without any trouble at all.

"Well, maybe another night then," she says.

"Sure, Mrs. Rockledge. That would be great."

"Hey, everyone. Did you see this?" Dad walks in the door from the driveway holding one of our car wash flyers.

"You put one in *my* mailbox?" I whisper to Tommy. I know Tommy is my best friend and all, but there are definitely days when I question his intelligence. I mean, first he volunteers us to work on the fundraising committee with Lisa, and then he puts a flyer for an event *I thought of* and am *helping to organize* in my own mailbox? Yeah, not the brightest of the bunch sometimes.

"Nathan, your school is having a car wash," Dad says. "What great timing! I was just saying the other day that I needed to get my car washed. Remember?"

"Yeah, Dad," I reply. "That's what gave me the idea. Our class is doing it. We're trying to raise money so we can go on the trip to New York City this spring. We need to raise a thousand dollars before winter break or the trip is off."

"Well a car wash is a great idea!" Dad says. "Hey, Nathan, did I ever tell you about the time Uncle Robert and I wanted to surprise Grandpop by washing his car?"

"You mean the time you used Grandmom's fancy bubble bath to scrub down the seats?" I ask.

"Yeah," Dad says, as his eyes glaze over. He stares out the window as if the memory is right outside. "Grandmom was not happy. She acted like that bubble bath was made of gold. We had to use all our allowance money to buy her a new bottle. Grandpop wasn't happy either. It took forever to get all the bubbles out of the upholstery. Plus, his seats smelled like raspberries for a year! Actually, it was quite pleasant, but Grandpop didn't like it one bit." Dad turns back around as he snaps out of his memory trance. "Anyway, I think having a car wash is a great idea, boys. You're sure to make a ton of money."

"I hope so," I say. "We're also doing an auction. Do you think any of the people you work with might have stuff to donate?"

"Wow, another great idea. I may have to hire you two boys for our own marketing department at work. Your ideas are much better than some of the stuff our people come up with, but don't tell them I said so. They're a little touchy when it comes to that sort of thing." Dad winks at us. "Anyway, I'll ask some of my clients tomorrow about the auction. They have all kinds of fancy stuff. I'm sure they'd love to help. "

"Thanks, Dad. We're going to make some flyers for the auction right now. Would you mind making copies when you're at work and passing them around?"

"Sounds good to me, Nathan."

"Cool. Well, we'd better get busy." Tommy and I run up the stairs and into my room with Bobino right on our trail.

"So what time is your aunt coming for dinner," I ask, as I grab some blank paper.

"Who?" Tommy asks. "Oh, um, she's not." He half smiles at me and shrugs his shoulders.

Chapter 14

Despite the cold, most of our class is here at school to help with the car wash today. Maybe having a car wash in November isn't the greatest idea after all. It's freezing out here. Not exactly the best day to be standing outside for hours, working with cold water. At least the sun is shining. Lisa was *supposed* to be in charge of planning a rain date, but she never did. She claims she was too busy getting all the supplies she needed for her ornaments. Lucky for us, it doesn't seem as though we'll need it.

Abby and Mom are selling hot chocolate. Thankfully, Mom didn't have enough time to make a big enough batch of her special homemade hot chocolate, so she had to settle for the packets of powder. All she needs to do is add hot water and stir. It's kind of hard to mess that up. Right?

Dad and some of the other parents are standing at the driveway of the school directing traffic. There are a surprisingly large number of cars already lined up, and we only just started. We've got four stations set up to help move things along. First cars enter the wash area. Then they move over to the rinse station and then the dry station before they move over to the final station set up to clean out their interiors.

We don't have any of those big fancy vacuums to do the insides of the cars, but we have big trashcans lined up for people who want us to help them throw away all their garbage and stuff. We call that the trash station. Clever, huh?

Mrs. Cogin is supervising and collecting the money. Lisa was collecting the money at first, but Mrs. Cogin moved her to the drying station after she gave the first person twenty dollars for their change instead of five. Lisa says the bills were sticking together, and she couldn't get them apart. Whatever. At least Tommy and I are not at the same station as Lisa. We are at rinsing for now. Mrs. Cogin says we'll all rotate every twenty minutes so we get to do a little of everything. It sure is cold out here, and the sun doesn't seem quite as bright as it was a minute ago. In fact, there are suddenly a lot more clouds than there were when we first got here. The wind has picked up a bit as well. I look over at Abby. She's drinking hot chocolate and talking to some teenage boy. Why am I not surprised? I really don't know why Mom insists on bringing her to all these things, she never does anything helpful anyway. We could actually use an extra hand over at the drying station. Lisa is slowing everything down. Next time Mrs. Cogin walks by, I think I'll mention that to her.

"Hey, Nathan. Pass me that rag, will you?" Tommy yells from the other side of the car we are rinsing off.

He finishes, and the next car pulls up. Lisa is still drying the same car she was drying five minutes ago. I don't understand why it takes her so long.

Drying is the easiest task in this entire process. We rinse another car, but have to wait for Lisa before any more cars can come through. Thank goodness we get to go to drying next. We'll be able to get the line moving again.

After what seems like much longer than twenty-minutes, Mrs. Cogin finally yells, "SWITCH!"

I gladly put down the cold hose. At least in the drying station my hands won't get all wet, and I can wear my gloves. Tommy and I move over as we wait for the owner of the car we were just rinsing to pull up. Lisa is still standing in the drying station, holding a rag.

"You're supposed to move to the next station," I tell her, as I pick up a clean, dry towel from the bucket.

"I don't want to," she says.

"It's not really optional," I explain. "We're supposed to rotate every twenty minutes, and Mrs. Cogin just yelled switch. Didn't you hear her? You need to move to the trash station."

Lisa crosses her arms in front of her body. "I'm not picking up other people's trash. It's unsanitary. You go over there. I'm not moving," she firmly states.

"Fine," I snap, really not in the mood to stand there and argue. "Come on, Tommy."

We walk over to where all the trashcans are set up. I have to agree with Lisa, picking up other people's trash isn't exactly the most fun job, but at least we're one step closer to the hot chocolate stand. Mrs. Cogin says that after we rotate through, we get to take a short break for hot cocoa. Oh well, I guess

Lisa won't be getting any since she refuses to move away from the drying station. That's her problem, not mine. The first car pulls up. It's a mess. There are food wrappers and papers everywhere. The owner helps us as we dig through, throwing all the trash away. When we're done, he gives Tommy and me an extra two dollars each as a tip. Hey, maybe being at the trash station isn't so bad after all.

The sound of a loud engine catches my attention. I watch as a bright orange sports car with yellow racing stripes pulls into the wash station. Cool! I can't wait to have that car in my station.

The next car pulls through. It's the one Tommy and I had rinsed off earlier. There isn't too much to clean on the inside, so we finish pretty quickly.

"I'm sorry, boys," the owner says, "I didn't bring any extra money with me to tip you."

"Oh," Tommy says, "it's okay. You don't need to tip us."

"No, I want to. You boys did a great job." He pulls out a piece of paper and a pen. "Here," he says, handing it to me, "write down your names, and I'll drop a little something off at the school for you on Monday."

The man starts telling Tommy all about how his own daughters went to our school when they were young and how he remembers them trying to raise money for the same school trip. Suddenly, the man's engine starts to roar, and the car takes off, with the owner still standing beside us.

"Hey!" the owner of the car yells. "That's my car! That man has just stolen my car!" He looks at me.

"Nate! You've got to do something! Go after him!"

"Me?" I ask. "But I don't drive! I'm only eleven!"

"Don't be ridiculous, Nate!" the man says, lowering the shield on my helmet. "You're the great Nate Rocks! Winner of last year's Speed Rally 500!"

I look down to see that I am wearing a bright orange and yellow racing suit.

"Please, Nate! Go! You've got to get my car back!" He nods his head in the direction of the orange and yellow racecar that pulled in earlier, engine already running.

I sprint over to the car, hop in through the open window, and rev up the engine. I speed off with screeching tires and a trail of smoke behind me. The stolen car carelessly weaves in and out of traffic up ahead of me. I push down on the accelerator even harder, making my way closer to him. Just as the stolen car is about to enter a busy intersection, it makes a sharp right down an alley. I follow closely behind as it speeds through and turns down another side road. I've got to figure out a way to cut this guy off. If he makes it back onto the main road, he will put a whole lot of people in danger.

The driver turns left, then right. I manage to get next to him, trying to push him off to the side, but he won't budge. We are now side by side, racing down a deserted dirt road. Pebbles and sand are flying everywhere as our tires push through, each trying to gain an edge on the other. The dirt road turns back to asphalt. In front of us, a sign reads, "Bridge Out 500 Feet." Oh no! If we keep going straight, we will wind up in the water, but if we turn, we will be heading into a busy intersection. I've got to stop this guy! Think, Nate, think!

I push on my accelerator as hard as it will go and turn my wheel sharply at the same time. I can feel the car tilting onto its two right side tires. Driving sideways, I slide by the other car and turn my wheel sharply again, this time in the other direction. My car slides to the front. My head hits the windshield as the car slams back down on to all fours, blocking the stolen car's path. The stolen car hits its brakes and swerves into the guardrail. Smoke spews from the front of the crumpled car. I can hear the sound of sirens quickly approaching as I slide myself back out of the racecar's window and over to the stolen car. The other driver punches his fists against the steering wheel in defeat.

Police cars come to a screeching halt. "Nate Rocks," one of the policemen says, as he runs over to me, "you did it! You caught our car thief! Another few feet and he would have crashed into the intersection. You saved many lives today, Nate."

I watch as the other policeman handcuffs the car thief and leads him to the back of his police car.

"You are a true hero," the policeman continues. He leans over and touches my forehead. "You've got a nasty cut on your head. Are you in any pain?"

"What?"

"Rain! I said rain! Nathan, why are you just standing there drawing on that paper? It's pouring out. We're closing down the car wash! We need to get inside now."

I shake the water away from my face as I look at my mom. Everyone except the man with the orange and yellow sports car is gone. He honks his horn and winks as he drives off.

Chapter 15

Lisa, Tommy, and I stare out the window watching the other kids play while we wait for Mrs. Cogin to arrive. It's time for our next fundraising meeting.

"If you and Tommy had rinsed faster," Lisa says, "we could have gotten more cars through."

"What?" I ask. Is she joking? "You were the one holding up the line. You were taking way too long to dry the cars. All you had to do was wipe them down and move them along."

"Please, Nathan, don't you know anything about washing cars? Drying is the most important step. If you don't do it properly, the cars will be all streaky. It's no wonder Mrs. Cogin had me stay at the drying station the whole time."

"You refused to move. Anyway, if we had a rain date set up like we were supposed to, we would have been open for more than an hour." I use an accusatory tone. I know I should be nicer. After all, Lisa was sick in bed for the rest of the weekend. It stunk for her, but actually worked out great for Tommy and me, because she was too sick to come with us to the mall on Sunday.

"I already told you!" Lisa screeches. "The school

didn't have any other dates available, and I had to go get all the supplies for the ornaments. Honestly, I don't know how you expected me to find another location on such short notice. Who has a car wash when it's so cold out anyway? Thanks to you I was sick all weekend." She crosses her arms in front of her chest and looks back out the window.

"Why thanks to me?" I ask.

She opens her eyes scary big and says, "*Because*, it was *your* idea to have the car wash in the freezing cold rain!"

"The weather was not my fault, and besides ..."

"All right," Mrs. Cogin says, walking into the room. "That's enough yelling. I could hear you all the way down the hall!" She pulls her chair next to us and continues. "Well, I'm sure you don't need me to tell you that we didn't quite make as much money as we hoped at the car wash."

"How much did we make?" Tommy asks.

Mrs. Cogin holds up a small stack of bills. "Twenty-nine dollars. Twenty-five from the car wash and four from hot chocolate sales."

I sit back and sigh. "So we still need...a lot," I say, trying to hide the fact that I can't figure out the math in my head.

"Nine-hundred and seventy-one to be exact," Lisa states smugly.

Show off.

"Yes," Mrs. Cogin agrees. "We really need to pull in some great items for the auction. Any ideas?"

"Nathan and I went to the mall yesterday," Tommy

says. "We passed out a bunch of flyers and asked people in different stores if they wanted to donate stuff to help." Tommy hands Mrs. Cogin one of the papers we made up.

"I like these. Good thinking, boys. Any luck?" she asks, while reading.

"Not really," I answer. "I mean, I'm not sure. Apparently store managers don't work on Sundays, but we did drop off a lot of the flyers."

"Don't forget, Nathan, we did get that one thing..." Tommy begins.

Okay, so the mall trip was kind of a waste and slightly embarrassing. Well, maybe more than slightly. Mom dropped Abby, Emma, Tommy, and me off first thing in the morning. Most of the stores weren't even open yet. It was mostly just a bunch of older people walking around the loops of each floor. Basically, people walking in circles. I'm not sure why. They looked pretty strange. I don't get why the mall would even be open if the stores were all closed. Maybe they were filming one of those hidden camera shows where they make fun of people. Yeah, that was probably it. They were probably thinking – let's fool people by opening the mall before the stores open so we can watch them walk in circles. Okay, that makes sense I guess. Cool. I'll have to watch for that episode. Lucky for us, we didn't fall for it. We all just headed to the food court to sit and wait. Abby and Emma wound up sitting across the room because they didn't want to be seen with a couple of fifth graders, which was just fine with me. It's not like I wanted to be seen with them either.

Anyway, once the stores and food stands started opening up, Tommy and I each got a soft pretzel and a slushy. Mine kind of, sort of, got knocked over and spilled on all the flyers. Thankfully, it was lemon, so you could still read the writing on the papers. It would have been much worse if Tommy had spilled his. He had cherry. I mopped them off best I could, but they were still wet and sticky.

We next headed over to the arcade, figuring the flyers needed some time to dry. Well, I guess we lost track of time because at some point, Abby appeared, snapping her gum, and telling us that Mom just called her to say she was on her way to pick us up. Tommy and I spent the next twenty minutes racing around the mall, where we did in fact learn that most store managers don't work on Sundays. We handed out almost all of the flyers to salespeople who didn't really seem to care. We were just getting ready to leave a gift store, when the person behind the counter offered us a ..."

"A photo frame?" Lisa asks, as Tommy pulls the box out of his book bag.

"Yeah," I reply. "What's wrong with a photo frame? I'll bet it will bring in plenty of bids."

"It won't sell for more than five dollars," Lisa says. "We need big stuff, stuff that has a wow factor. Stuff that people wouldn't normally think about buying." She shakes her head in disgust.

"Well it's a good start, but Lisa is right. We do need

some bigger ticket items," Mrs. Cogin explains. "I have to go bring the others in from recess. This afternoon we'll spend some time making new flyers and posters so the entire class can get involved in bringing in donations. Don't worry, I have a good feeling we'll get exactly what we need."

We watch in silence as Mrs. Cogin leaves the room. Once we can no longer hear her heels clicking down the hall, Lisa squints her eyes at Tommy and me, and says, "I can't believe it. An entire day at the mall, and that's all you got?"

"Well, yeah," Tommy says, "but we dropped flyers off in every store, so I'm sure as soon as the managers see them they'll start contacting us. Plus, Nathan's dad is going to ask some of his clients for stuff, isn't that right, Nathan?"

I nod.

"Besides, what did you get for the auction?" Tommy leans over and stares at Lisa directly in her eyes.

It's not often Tommy lets Lisa have it, but he was all excited to tell Mrs. Cogin about that picture frame, and now I can tell he is mad. Let 'em rip, Tommy!

"So far all you've done is complain, Lisa," Tommy starts. "Nathan here is the one who came up with the ideas for the car wash *and* the auction. All you've got is your dumb old ornaments."

Yeah, Tommy! You tell her!

"Dumb?! I thought you said they were a good idea!" Lisa yells.

Tommy smirks at her. "I was just trying to be nice. Did you seriously think you could make a thousand dollars selling ornaments? What a joke."

Tommy stops talking as we hear the rest of the class coming back in. He sits back in his chair, looking satisfied. For once, Lisa did not get the last word.

"Class, settle down quickly," Mrs. Cogin starts. "The fundraising committee met this afternoon, and well, as I'm sure you all figured out, we did not make as much money at the car wash as we were hoping."

Tommy coughs and says "rain date" at the same time. Looks like he's not quite done with Lisa just yet. Mrs. Cogin gives him her *warning* look, and Tommy clears his throat. "Sorry," he says. "I think I'm just catching that cold that's been going around."

"As I was saying," Mrs. Cogin continues, "while the car wash may not have been the success we were hoping for, we still have the auction coming up in a few weeks. It is important that we all work together to make this happen. So I have an assignment for you all. Nathan and Tommy have already passed around flyers in the mall. I need each of you to follow up with the stores there before the end of the week. You can work in pairs if you like. I will split the stores up and give you your assignment by the end of the day. You can either call them or visit them, but either way, I want you to try to get them to commit to giving us an item for the auction. I'd also like you all to find two additional places where you can request donations. For example, Nathan asked his dad to check around at work. Bring a list of all donated items back here on Friday. Remember, you are representing our school. You need to look presentable, be polite, and smile."

"I guess that leaves Lisa out," Tommy snickers. We high five and look up just in time to receive Mrs. Cogin's warning look number two.

Chapter 16

Tommy and I pair up, of course. We are assigned two stores in the mall to re-visit: the store where they sell all the cool signed sports stuff and the sneaker store. They happen to be two of my favorite stores. I guess Mrs. Cogin took pity on us since Tommy and me already did a lot of the work already. Well, some of the work...well, more work than anyone else had done. I mean we did make the first batch of flyers, and we did go to the mall with good intentions. Nobody needs to know that we barely spent any time trying to get donations. Okay, so *trying* might be stretching it a little. We sort of ran into each store, asked the person working to give the flyer to the manager, and ran out to the next store. We got the ball rolling though, and that's what counts.

The other fifth grade class is helping too, so Sam is able to team up with Tommy and me as well. Since Mom has some shopping she wants to do, she decides to take us to the mall after school on Wednesday. We only have a half hour, so we agree we will skip the slushies, pretzels, and arcade this time and get right to work instead. Tommy had done some investigative work beforehand and knew that the managers of both the stores on our list were working that afternoon. See that? I always knew Tommy was a smart one!

As soon as we get to the mall, Mom leaves us. She says she wants to go over to the cooking store for some big sale they are having or something. I sure hope they are selling some cooking lessons. That would be awesome.

"So what are we going to say?" Tommy asks, as we head in the direction of the sports store.

"I don't know," I reply, "I haven't really thought about it. Maybe we should jot down some notes."

We stop at one of the benches to sit and think for a moment. I turn over a flyer and grab a pen out of my back pocket. Hmmm ... what should we say, what should we say, what should we ...

"I'll tell you what you should say," an unfamiliar voice states.

"What?" I ask. "Who are you? Where did Tommy and Sam go?"

"Tommy and Sam who? Oh never mind about that, Nate. I'm the mall manager, and you've got to come quickly. We need your help!"

"Me? Wait. How do you know my name?"

"Why you're Nate Rocks, of course! Everyone knows your name. Listen, I don't have time to go all fan gaga over you right now. I need your help! Are you coming or what?"

"Uh sure," I reply, trying to keep up with the man as he quickly walks through the first floor of the mall. "So what's the problem?"

"You know the arcade next to Carl's Music Corner?"

"Sure, my friends and I love it there. What about it?"

"Well, it's closing, and Carl wants to rent out the space. He wants to take down the wall and expand his store. He's meeting with the owner of the mall right now. You've got to stop him, Nate! We can't have a mall without a video arcade."

The mall manager looks like he is about to cry as he explains the situation to me. I can't say I really blame him.

"That's horrible! But what can I do?" I ask.

"I don't know, Nate, but you've got to do something, and fast! We don't have a lot of time!"

I follow the man through a doorway that I never noticed before, not that I pay much attention to stuff in the mall—other than the arcade that is. We walk through a passageway that runs behind all of the stores. I wonder how many other secret passageways there are in this mall. The hallway twists and turns so many times, I've lost track of where I am or how to get back. We finally stop in front of a set of dark wood double doors.

"Well," the mall manager says, "this is it for me. Good luck, Nate."

"What?" I ask, as the man opens the doors and pushes me inside. "Wait," I say, but the doors slam shut behind me.

"Wait for what?" asks a man sitting behind a desk, presumably the man who owns the mall. "I don't have time to wait, son. I'm trying to close a deal here."

I look over to another man sitting in a chair on the

other side of the desk.

"Are you Carl?" I ask. "From Carl's Music Corner?"

"I am," he says. "Look, I'm sorry, but it's like I've been telling the kids all day. I'm sold out of the new Desmond Harper CD. You'll just have to wait until the shipment comes in sometime next week." He looks back over to the man behind the desk— Mr. Mall Owner. "Sorry about that. These kids have been driving me nuts with all this Desmond Harper nonsense. His CD sold out in the first day. I personally don't get it. To me it's just a bunch of noise and screeching that they call singing, but you know how these kids can be. One day they're ..."

"Can we get on with this please?" Mr. Mall Owner interrupts. He pushes a paper across his desk and towards Carl.

"Oh, sorry. I guess I got a little carried away there. So where do I sign?"

"Wait!" I yell. "Please, wait!"

Both men look up at me.

"Please," I continue. I walk slowly over to the desk. "Sir, with all due respect, you can't get rid of the arcade. You just can't!"

"Of course I can!" Mr. Mall Owner exclaims. "That arcade has been nothing but a money sucker. Plus, it only attracts troublemakers to our mall. I'll tell you what, I'm happy to see it finally go."

"But sir, it's the best part of the mall. Why I love coming here on the weekends to hangout, er, I mean spend money at the arcade. My friends and I have a great time...spending money there. Afterwards we go to the food court where we spend more money, and then we go shopping at cool stores like Carl's Music Corner where we spend even more money. If it weren't for the arcade, we wouldn't have a reason to come to the mall. We'd buy all our music from Tunes To Go over on 73rd Street."

Carl gasps. "Tunes To Go? Oh my! Well, we can't have that happen, now can we?" he remarks.

I walk in front of Carl to block his view from Mr. Mall Owner.

"Mr. Carl, sir," I say, "that arcade is filled with a lifetime of memories for me and my friends."

"Uh, kid, what are you…like ten or eleven or something? Now get on out of here. You're wasting our time," Mr. Mall Owner says.

"Well now hold on a second. Maybe we should give him a chance," Carl says, "I would actually like to hear what this fine young fellow has to say."

"Thank you, sir," I reply. "I'll never forget my very first game of Zebra Hop. It was right here in this mall. I was only five or six years old. My dad brought me down to the arcade while my mom took my sister to get new shoes. It was magical I tell you, listening to all the sounds from the different machines. And the flashing lights! I felt like I was in a dream. I couldn't take my eyes off the giant game with the talking zebra on it. I begged my dad for a chance to play it. All you had to do was get the zebra to the other side of the street by avoiding all the obstacles. Dad finally gave in. I could barely reach the controls, so he had to pick me up. I remember trying so hard to get that zebra across the street safely, but every time I got close to the other side—SLAM—a pickup truck would come out of nowhere and flatten that poor zebra right out. But my dad didn't let me give up. No sir. He kept putting quarters into the machine, telling me I could do it. Before I knew it, there was a whole crowd around me cheering me on. Everyone in that arcade was rooting for me to get that zebra across. I looked up at all the encouraging faces, all the people who wanted me to succeed, and do you know what happened?"

Carl wipes the tears from his eyes. "You got the zebra across the street?"

"No," I say, "I didn't. My mom showed up and yelled at my dad for spending all that money and made us leave, but that's not important. What's important is that on that day, I learned never to give up. I'm still trying to get that darn zebra across the street, sir. If you close the arcade, I'll have to give up my dream."

"Oh for goodness sake," Mr. Mall Owner says. "Are you going to sign the contract or not, Carl?"

"Yup!" Carl says. He grabs the paper and pen and signs his name at the bottom of the paper.

I sadly shake my head. I really thought my speech changed his mind.

"Congratulations, Carl! You are now the proud owner of space #46. Formerly known as The Arcade, and the future home of the newly expanded Carl's Music Corner. So when do you want to start knocking down walls? We can probably get a crew out here to start work on Monday if that works for you," Mr. Mall Owner says.

I start walking toward the door. No point in me

staying to hear anymore.

"I won't be knocking down any walls," Carl says. "The arcade stays!"

I spin around. The double doors burst open. The mall manager runs in. "You did it, Nate! You did it! I knew you would. Thank you so much. You saved our arcade!"

"I don't know what to say," Mr. Mall Owner mumbles.

"Did you hear me, Nathan? I asked what should we say," Tommy repeats. "Why are you drawing zebras all over that paper? I thought you were going to write down some stuff that we could tell the store managers."

"Don't worry, Tommy, I've got this. We'll tell them it's for the sake of the children. Grown-ups love a sappy story. Trust me, it gets them every time."

Chapter 17

Our mall trip went better than expected. The sports store gave us a uniform jersey with the name of my favorite Phillies player on the back, and the sneaker store gave us a fifty dollar gift certificate. Both store managers insisted on waiting for Mom to come in before handing over the goods. I guess they didn't trust us or something. Not that the thought of keeping that jersey for myself didn't cross my mind, 'cause it did. Mom must have been worried about that too, because she took it straight over to the school first thing the next morning. I sure hope Mom and Dad bid on that jersey for me.

Dad was able to get some donations from his work clients as well. Boring things, like passes to some fancy play in the city and tickets to the ballet. No thanks. I'll stick to the baseball stuff. The other kids at school got some neat items also, like movie DVDs and video games. It was looking like we might actually be able to raise $971 after all.

The auction is in just a few hours. Of course, Mom volunteered all of us to be on the committee to help set everything up, and of course, Abby is in the corner sulking and texting. Just another typical day for the Rockledge family. Tommy, Lisa, and their families are helping as well.

Tommy and I are setting up the folding chairs and putting numbered paper paddles on each seat for people to raise when they want to bid on something. Thankfully, Lisa is not with us. Mrs. Cogin has her setting up her ornament table along the back wall of the gym. At first, Lisa complained that her ornaments should be up front with all the auction items, but when she figured out that every person had to walk by her table to get to their seats, she decided she liked her spot after all.

Mom, Tommy's mom, and Marge, Lisa's mom, are setting up the food table. By some strange miracle, Mom wound up not having time to bake anything, so she asked Tommy's mom to be in charge of food. For once, I'm not afraid of the snack table at a school event. It's lucky for the auction goers, too. We want them spending their money, not clutching their stomachs in agony.

"Hey, Nathan, Tommy," Dad calls over, as we get the last of the chairs set up. "Can you give me a hand?"

"Sure, Dad, what's up?"

"I can't get this easel to stay up," he says. "Can you hold it steady for me? I think it just needs a dab of glue." He pulls a small tube from his pants pocket.

"You carry glue around with you?" I ask.

"Sure, Nathan," he says. "Besides, this isn't just any glue, it's Magic Glue. Anything that touches it sticks instantly. It can pretty much fix anything. You just have to make sure you don't get any on your hands or they'll stick together, too!" He dabs a drop on the wood, and the easel stays up, no problem.

"It really is magic," Tommy whispers.

"Here." Dad puts the cap back on and hands the tube to me. "Would you mind holding it for me for a second? I want to go wash up before show time." I slide the glue into my pocket.

Dad volunteered to be the auctioneer; that's the guy who calls out all the prices. He's very excited. A little too excited if you ask me. All week long he's been practicing in this really weird voice where he barely opens his mouth and talks super fast. Yesterday at dinner, when I asked for more apple juice, he took my glass and blurted out all in one breath, "Apple juice is now on the table. Who's gonna start the bidding? I've got five, five, five! Do I hear ten? Thank you, sir, we've got ten. Now twenty, twenty, and thirty. Can I get thirty-five? Thirty-five, now forty, do I have forty? Anyone? Going once, going twice, last call, sold. Forty to the sharp looking boy in row four." Lucky for me I wasn't choking or anything. I could have wound up dead.

As the time for the auction approaches, the rest of the fifth grade class starts to show up. Everyone has a job. Some kids will be at the doors to greet the guests and sign them in, some will show people to their seats, some will help keep track of bids and record the winners. Tommy and I are stationed behind one of the auction tables. We're supposed to make sure the items stay on the table until they are called up to the front of the room for bidding.

"Everyone gather round," Mrs. Cogin says once everything is set up. "I'd like to thank you all for volunteering your time this afternoon. The gym looks like a real auction house. You all did a great job preparing for this event. Now I've been watching the weather, and it looks like this blizzard they are predicting is going to miss us, thank goodness, so I expect a big turnout. Are we ready? Cars are already starting to pull into the parking lot. Good luck fifth-graders. I think this auction is going to be a huge success!"

We all start cheering as Mrs. Cogin opens the doors. Within minutes, people start entering the gym, I mean, auction house. They spend the first twenty minutes walking around to all the tables to examine the items that are for sale. An awful lot of people are stopping to look at that baseball jersey I really want. I sure hope Mom remembers she promised to bid on it for me. She told me earlier, that if she won it, she would put it away for a Christmas present.

Dad bangs his gavel on the podium several times to get everyone's attention. "Please take your seats everyone, we're about to begin."

Mrs. Cogin brings the first item to Dad. A four pack of movie passes. "Ah," Dad says, "our first item of the afternoon, a lovely envelope containing four tickets to any movie of your choice playing over at the Cineplex on State Street. Yes, ladies and gentlemen, you can see a western, a comedy, a horror flick, or a sci-fi. Gentleman, you can bring your dates to see a romantic comedy on Valentine's Day or bring the little ones to see an animated movie. Perhaps they'll even have something in 3-D or you can go traditional and stay with the 2-D version, which is my personal preference. Those 3-D movies just give me a big old headache. In fact, the last time I went to a 3-D movie—"

"Um, Mr. Rockledge?" Mrs. Cogin interrupts.

"Yes, Mrs. Cogin?" Dad replies.

"We've got over fifty items to get through. Maybe we could just give a one line description and get right to the bidding?"

"Oh, sure. Sure," Dad answers. "Okay, let's start the bidding."

The items are selling, but they do not seem to be selling for very much money. The movie passes sell for only twenty-five dollars, and the sneaker gift certificate sells for only thirty. I'm beginning to think we should have just asked for money donations from all these places instead of items. Worst of all, my jersey sold for a measly seventy-five dollars. It was worth over a hundred. Mom didn't even bid on it; she was too busy with the snack table. Some guy wearing big goofy sunglasses wound up winning it. Who wears sunglasses inside? He probably doesn't even like baseball.

Dad calls for an intermission. Outside, heavy snow is starting to come down. I guess that blizzard isn't going to miss us after all.

"Hey, Dad." I motion for him to come over to the table where I am standing.

"It's going well, Nathan, don't you think?" he asks, still holding the gavel.

"Dad," I begin, "this is all that's left." I tilt my head toward the table. "Do you think we're going to make enough money?"

"I don't know," Dad says. He looks up out the window. "It's starting to snow pretty hard. People are going to want to leave soon to get home before the roads get bad. Let's make a list of everything that is left. Maybe we can offer the higher priced items first."

"Good idea, Dad. I'll run to my classroom for some paper and a pen."

As I walk back towards the gymnasium, the lights begin to flicker. I'm about halfway there, when the lights go out completely, leaving me standing in the pitch dark.

"Nate! Nate! Come quickly, we need your help!"

I see someone with a flashlight running toward me.

"Mrs. Simmons, is that you?"

"Yes, Nate. You must come with me, we have no time to waste!"

"What's wrong?" I ask. "Why did all the lights go out?"

"It's the storm," Mrs. Simmons says. "But we have bigger problems. It seems that the doors to the gym are stuck. No one can get in or out. We have to get them open before people realize they are locked inside and things get ugly."

"Why are the doors stuck?" I ask. This whole thing just is not making sense to me.

Mrs. Simmons continues, "Nate, the gym doors are electric, and when the power goes down, they don't work. Honestly, didn't you learn anything about electricity in science class? Anyway, for some reason the emergency safety latch is not working."

"Shouldn't we call 9-1-1?" I ask. "They can send over the fire department. They have those big axes, and they can cut right through those doors. Ooh, do you think they'll let me swing the axe? That would be so awesome."

"Nate! Listen to me. We can't call 9-1-1. The phone lines aren't working either. Please, Nate, you've got to help me get the doors open and fast, before there is an all out panic. People do crazy things once they get into a panic! They start yelling and screaming and even get violent," Mrs. Simmons cries, as she roughly shakes my shoulders.

"You're telling me," I mumble, as I try to release her grip. "Follow me."

We race down the hallway toward the gym. People are already starting to pound on the door.

"Don't worry," Mrs. Simmons tries to yell over the sound, "we're trying to fix the doors."

"Where is the emergency latch?" I ask.

Mrs. Simmons shines her flashlight up. Above the door is a small pass through window that is open a tiny crack. The metal latch hangs on the other side of the window just above the door with a piece of rope dangling down toward the ground. The metal latch is split in two.

If only I could figure out a way to get that latch back together. Think, Nate, think. That's it! I pull the glue Dad had given me earlier in the day out of my pocket and read the label: Bonds metal instantly.

"Mrs. Simmons," I ask, "is there a ladder around? I think I can fix the latch, but I'll have to go through that window up there."

"Nate," she says. "I can't let you do that! You'll hurt yourself!"

"Mrs. Simmons, it's the only way. I'm the only one small enough to fit through there." I run into the nearest classroom and drag a desk and chair out into the hallway and over to the gym door. I carefully stack the chair onto the desk and start climbing.

Mrs. Simmons holds the chair steady for me. "Careful, Nate, please!"

My legs wobble as I climb up onto the chair. I can barely reach the window. Holding the tube of glue in my teeth, I use both hands to pull myself up and through the window, balancing my stomach on the window's edge. The room below me goes silent.

The gym is not as dark as the hallway thanks to several sets of windows way up high above the basketball nets. In fact, I can see pretty clearly.

Mom pushes her way through the crowd.

"Be careful, Nathan, please!" she yells.

I unscrew the top of the tube and squeeze the glue out onto one of the pieces of metal, being extra cautious not to get any on my fingers.

"Easy, Nathan," I hear Dad say, "you can do this, son. I have faith in you."

I reach for the other piece of metal and attach it gently to the first piece of metal that has the glue. I hold my breath and let go. The two pieces are still together. Dad gives me the thumbs up.

"Dad," I say, "count to twenty after I get down and pull on the rope. It should release the doors."

I slide back out the window. Mrs. Simmons

continues to hold the chair and desk steady as I make my way down. I push the furniture out of the way just in time to hear a loud *click*. The doors open up and everyone cheers. Mom runs over to me, hugging me, and the crowd opens up to let me walk through.

The man with the sunglasses, the one who won the Phillies jersey, walks over to me. He takes off his shades, and my mouth drops open. "It's you!" I say in astonishment.

Abby walks next to me. "Who?"

I look at Abby. "Abby, are you kidding me? This is only the greatest first baseman the Phillies have ever had." I stick out my trembling hand. "I-it's nice to meet you, sir."

"The pleasure is mine, Nathan," he says. "What you did here today, well it was amazing. You are a true hall of famer in my book."

"Thank you, sir," I say, my voice still shaky. I look down to see him holding the uniform jersey he bought earlier in auction. "You bought your own jersey?" I ask.

"Nathan, the owner of the sports store in the mall contacted my manager after you and your friend stopped by. He told my manager all about your school trip and wanted to see if I was interested in signing something to auction off. I thought it was a great idea. I remember trying to raise money when I was a kid to go to sports camp. It wasn't easy, but thanks to some really generous people, I was able to go. Now it's my turn to help. Anyway, I thought I would buy the jersey, sign it, and then offer it back into the auction." The ball player holds the jersey up against the wall and signs his name across the back.

"Wow," Tommy says, eyes wide open.

"Except, I've changed my mind," the baseball player says.

"You have?" I ask, completely confused.

The ball player slips the signed jersey over my head. "This is for you, Nathan. My gift to you for being so brave."

"For me?" I ask in disbelief. "Whoa."

"Yes, and for the school, I will personally write a check to cover the cost of the trip."

Everyone in the room cheers. The ball player raises his hands to quiet everyone down.

"One more thing," he says. "Your principal was kind enough to give me the dates for your New York trip. It just so happens that we'll be in New York for a game then, and I've got tickets for the entire fifth grade."

Tommy and I look at each other and smile. New York City is going to ROCK!

Books by Karen Pokras Toz:

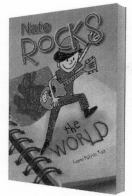

Nate ROCKS the WORLD

Nate ROCKS the BOAT

MILLICENT MARIE IS NOT MY NAME

Available at fine bookstores everywhere.

ACKNOWLEDGEMENTS

As I sat down to write this third Nate Rocks book, I began to think about all of the wonderful people who really helped get my books off the ground. Without them, Nate, as well as his family and friends, would all just be hanging out in my head causing all kinds of trouble!

A big thank you goes to my parents for all of their love, support, and encouragement, and for sending out mass emails to all of their awesome friends every time I publish a book.

As always, I need to thank my husband and children, who I think are finally getting used to the fact that I'm way behind on the laundry and have given up on cooking gourmet meals. I'd like to be able to tell them that this will someday change, but it probably won't. So to my family: Thank you for loving me as is.

Thank you to my fabulous group of beta readers and early reviewers for giving me your time and your honest feedback: Jane Anne Linsdell, Jaime Hope, Amanda Beatty Chambers, Wendy Nystrom, Stacey Rourke, and Jessica Haight. These wonderful people are not only readers and reviewers, but also they are talented writers and bloggers. Please take some time to check out their works.

To my editor, Melissa Ringsted – I so appreciate your

talents. Thank you for teaching, listening, and especially for understanding Nate's voice. I look forward to working on my next project with you.

To Deana Riddle, my outstanding cover artist, interior formatter, and general book go-to guru. Thank you so much for these amazing covers, for bringing life to my characters, and for all of your much-needed advice. I know you cringe every time I say, "let's try..." but I truly do love working with you.

And last, but definitely not least, thank you to my incredible readers. This was supposed to be the last book in the series, but because of your kind words, Nate Rocks continues on. I'm thrilled that you love reading Nate's adventures as much as I love writing them. Keep reading - you all rock!

xoxo~Karen

If you enjoyed Nate's Halloween adventure in chapters 7 and 8, be sure to check out the Anchor Group Anthology: *Paranormal Days Gone Awry*, where you can find *Nate Rocks the Wand* as well as 12 other exciting short stories by various authors.

18464068R00084

Made in the USA
San Bernardino, CA
15 January 2015